CASCADIA WOLVES: ENFORCER

LAUREN DANE

ELLORA'S CAVE
ROMANTICA PUBLISHING

What the critics are saying...

ఐ

"Lauren Dane's Cascadia Wolves: *Enforcer* is a scorching-hot pager turner!" ~ *The Romance Studio Reviews*

"Ms. Dane allows readers to jump right into the story, rather than spending a lot of time explaining the hierarchy of the packs, instead describing them as they come up, which allows for a more action-packed tale." ~ *Romance Review Today*

"*Enforcer* kept me enthralled throughout. With a well written plot, plenty of action," ~ *Euro Reviews*

"ENFORCER is the fantastic start of a new series and this reviewer looks forward to read many more books about the Cascadians!" ~ *Love Romances*

"*Enforcer* offers readers an action-packed plot, tantalizing passion, emotional struggles, and an unknown dangerous element in the middle of it all." ~ *Fallen Angel Reviews*

An Ellora's Cave Romantica Publication

www.ellorascave.com

Enforcer

ISBN 9781419958311
ALL RIGHTS RESERVED.
Enforcer Copyright © 2006 Lauren Dane
Edited by Ann Leveille.
Cover art by Syneca.

This book printed in the U.S.A. by Jasmine-Jade Enterprises, LLC.

Electronic book Publication April 2006
Trade paperback Publication October 2008

ENFORCER

∽

Dedication

∞

As always, Ray if you weren't in my life I wouldn't have all of these wonderful heroes in my head. You're everything. I love you.

To my wonderful beta readers: You all rock my world. Thanks for all your hard work!

To the most wonderful Ann Leveille – thank you so much for "getting" me and helping me to be the best writer I can.

Mom and Dad – I love you.

Trademarks Acknowledgement

∞

The author acknowledges the trademarked status and trademark owners of the following wordmarks mentioned in this work of fiction:

BMW: Bayerischemotoren Yerischemortoren Werke Aktiengesellschaft Corporation

Doc Marten: Dr. Martens International Trading

Harley: H-D Michigan, Inc.

He-man: Mattel, Inc.

Lassie: Golden Books Publishing Company, Inc.

Mercedes: DaimlerChrysler AG

Piaget: S.A. Ancienne Fabrique Geroges Piaget ET Cie.

Scooby: Hanna-Barbera Productions, Inc.

Smith &Wesson: Smith & Wesson Corp.

Velcro: Velcro Industries B.V Ltd.

Prologue
ಬಿ

"What the heck, Tommie? I got places to go, man," Rey said, fingers agitatedly drumming on the steering wheel.

Tommie Perkins flipped his friend the bird. "Dude, hold your horses. It's not like you got a woman or anything." He snorted in amusement at himself. "I have to check something out for Cade. Something big is going on, Reyes. It's got the hierarchy all shaken up and Lex is more nervous and paranoid than usual."

Rey snorted but kept driving. If his Alpha had business that needed tending to, he couldn't just blow it off. Even he had a sense of duty.

Tommie looked down at the scribbled address on the paper in his hand and back at the street signs. "Make a right into that parking lot. I'm going to be across the street. It shouldn't take me more than ten or fifteen minutes."

Gabriel Reyes pulled the dark sedan into the lot and parked it. He sat in the car, smoking a cigarette, and waited while Tommie ran inside to do his business. After a while he got bored listening to the radio and he made a few calls, but no one was around.

Checking his watch, he narrowed his eyes when he saw that twenty minutes had passed and still Tommie hadn't returned. It would serve the jerk-off right if he just left him. Rey got out of the car, sucked in a deep breath of the night air and heaved an annoyed sigh when he saw Tommie talking with some men he couldn't quite see in the doorway of one of the buildings.

He resolved to make the other man buy him a beer as he watched Tommie running toward him. As he got a few feet from the car, a shot rang out and Tommie looked up at him as he clutched his side with surprised agony.

Rey saw his lips form "*run*" just before another shot rang out and hit his friend in the head. "Jesus!" he cried out, jumping back into the car. He made quick work of turning the car on, squealing out of the parking lot, heading to Bellevue, where his sister lived. She'd know what to do.

Chapter One

෨

Annoyed, Lex Warden snapped his cell phone shut and let out a long breath as he took in the small cottage-style house. Once he pulled his bike onto the stand and got off, he dropped the helmet on the seat and ran his fingers through his hair to get rid of the helmet head he was sure he had after all that time riding over.

The house was light blue and someone obviously took great care of it. The lawn was neat and window boxes overflowed in a burst of red and white, standing out in colorful relief against the blue. There were raised beds along the front walk and a climbing rose snaked up a lattice off the front porch.

On the porch, a glider swing and a small table with a citronella candle. More pots of flowers and hanging baskets of greenery decorated the space. It was like a nice bit of the wild right there in the city. It gave the place a sense of calm, of refuge.

Shrugging off his amazement that anyone related to Gabriel Reyes could have such a neat and organized house, he stalked to the front door. Bypassing the doorbell, he pounded.

Moments later a tall, dark-haired woman answered and her eyes widened as she took him in.

Nina felt her mouth water as she got a load of the man standing on her porch. He was quite a specimen — well over six feet tall, blond-brown hair, deep green eyes. She swept her eyes down. His T-shirt and jeans were deceiving, they looked worn and faded but she could tell they were both designer, and the boots looked handmade. A gold Piaget watch decorated his wrist. Jeez, his hands were huge. She had to gather herself mentally as her normally ruthlessly tied down libido roared to life. She could feel her pulse flutter and she gave herself a hard mental smack. If there was one thing in the world Nina could recognize, it was trouble. And this guy was trouble. She'd placed herself on a trouble-free diet years before and she reminded herself that he was way off the menu.

Lex raked his glance over her from head to toe. The woman, most likely the sister, had on a white blouse buttoned up to the chin and slacks with low-heeled shoes. Her hair was tightly bound up into a bun on the top of her head and she was wearing glasses. He dismissed her as a sexual being immediately. "I'm looking for Rey." His voice was blunt, manner straightforward and slightly threatening.

She gathered herself up and stood tall, back straight. "Why?"

"Why?"

"Did I mumble? You do seem to speak English. Are you having a problem with the word? Do I need to explain it to you?"

Lex barely held back a growl of annoyance. "Listen, I'm looking for Rey. It doesn't have anything to do with you. Is he here or not?"

She raised a brow but remained silent, her arms crossed over her chest.

He tried to stare her down but she just snorted and started to step back and close her door in his face. "I need to talk to him," he added quickly. He shifted his weight from foot to foot, feeling like he'd been called to the principal's office.

"Is that so? He's not here. If you want to leave him a note, I'll give it to him when I see him next." Again, she started to close the door, but he put a hand out to stop her.

"When's that gonna be?"

"Just who *are* you?" Suspicious irritation was clear on her face as she examined him again, this time with a more critical eye.

"I'm Lex Warden. A friend of his."

Understanding lit her eyes, which she narrowed at him. Lex knew for sure this wasn't a good thing.

"No you're not. I know who you are, Mr. Warden, and you are not Gabriel's friend. He's had enough people in his life leading him astray. I should know, I've cleaned up after him long enough. Get the hell off my porch and don't bother coming back." She moved her arm behind the door.

He leaned in, growling, "Listen, lady, you don't know what you're getting in the middle of."

She poked him hard in the middle of his chest. Her face was hard, gaze furious. "You did *not* just growl at me! You listen here, I don't care what the fuck you want. Don't you dare try to intimidate me with your size! Growl at me! How dare you! Get the heck out of here and do it now before I shoot you."

He'd been fascinated with her face—at the light of ferocity in her eyes, the scent of a woman in full battle mode. He stepped forward only to feel something hard poke him in the balls. He looked down and saw the shotgun she pointed at him with her free hand. With horrified fascination, he watched as she used the hand she'd poked him with to pump the gun. He heard the unmistakable click of the ammo loading. All the while, the muzzle of the gun never left the region of his balls.

She didn't stand like a woman unused to a gun. He slid his glance back up into her face, where he met her determined and bloodthirsty gaze and felt a burst of heat bloom in his gut at the sight.

Despite his annoyance and yes, a bit of fear, he had to admit that she turned him on too. He put his hands up in surrender and took a step back. "Whoa! Let's not be hasty here. I don't want to hurt you. I don't want to hurt Rey either but I need to talk to him."

"I'm not hasty." She moved the shotgun tighter against his balls. "Test me why don't you? This is ready to roll and

I've had a shitty day." She narrowed her left eye at him and her lips—very nice lips, he noticed—curled up at one side in a grin.

"Look, wolf boy, he's gone. He came by, borrowed money," she snorted, "took money—it's not like I'll ever see it again—and headed out. Told me that the Pack was looking for him, wanting to kill him. Even if I knew where he ran to, which I don't, I certainly wouldn't tell someone out to hurt him."

"I told you, I'm not gonna hurt him. I need to talk to him." *Wolf boy?* He tried his sexy smile, a smile that this frigid-looking spinster should appreciate.

"Yeah, I'm sure that works on all the puppies down at the shelter. But I don't know you from Adam and the fact that you *say* you don't want to hurt him means nothing to me."

"Come on, Ms. Reyes. Give me a break. We can help each other out here, don't you think? We can talk about it more over dinner." He cocked his head in that adorable little boy way that his mother always melted over despite the puppies at the shelter comment.

She actually rolled her eyes at him and slammed the door in his face.

"Shit!" he hissed and walked back down the sidewalk to where his bike was parked. Casting a glance back at the house, he saw that the spinster was looking at him from the front windows. He tipped an imaginary hat at her as he put the key in and turned the ignition, firing the bike to life. He grunted a surprised laugh when she flipped him off in return.

* * * * *

Nina Reyes watched the man roar away on the Harley and closed the curtains with a sigh. Men were all the same, even if they were freaking werewolves. Okay, delicious hunks of hot, gorgeous hard werewolf flesh that she'd love to take a ride on. Oh, did she think that out loud? She winced and reminded herself that she had a battery-operated boyfriend and that was the best kind. No fuss, no muss and it never asked to borrow money.

With a snort, she put the shotgun back on the rack and removed the pins holding her hair in place. Chocolate brown curls shimmered down her back. She took off the clear lens glasses and placed them on the table near the door and rubbed her eyes.

She knew that she had the kind of looks that people remembered—long curly hair, big hazel eyes, long legs and full breasts. So she put her hair up in a severe bun. She'd cut it once but it just accentuated her eyes so she'd given herself the pleasure of letting it stay long, even if she was the only one who ever saw it down. She wore fake glasses and buttoned her shirts to the neck and wore slacks and flat shoes. It was necessary not to call attention to herself.

She wished her brother had the same caution. Damn that Gabriel! She couldn't believe he'd gotten her into yet another mess, and this time with werewolves. It was bad enough when he'd gotten attacked in a bar fight and had contracted the lycanthropy virus. She'd stood by him, hoping that surviving the adversity would make him stronger. He'd gotten involved with the local wolf Pack and had pretty much faded from her life. She'd gotten a card here and there, he'd borrowed money a few times, but she really didn't know much about his life. And with Gabriel, no news was good news. When she didn't get calls for bail at two in the morning she took it as a sign that he was alive and well, or at least not getting caught at whatever he was doing.

But really the change had only made a morally weak man physically stronger. It wasn't altogether surprising when, out of the blue, he'd showed up on her doorstep the night before, looking like the devil himself was chasing him. He said he'd seen something he wasn't supposed to and that the Pack was going to be looking for him to kill him for it. He'd certainly seemed scared for his life. She'd begged him to call the cops but he'd only looked at her like she was crazy. In the end, she'd given him all of the cash she had on her and in her emergency kitty and he'd gone, begging her to cover for him.

Cover for him! She snorted. Cover for him with frick-fracken werewolves. She rolled her eyes. But he was her brother, all the family she had, and she couldn't very well just let him get killed, even if he was a turd.

No, she was all he had and that meant something to her still. He was hers, for better or for worse, and she'd haul his ass out of trouble again, if only so she could give it a swift kick.

Double checking to be sure she'd locked the doors—as if that could stop a werewolf—she shrugged and reached back to grab the shotgun and headed for bed.

* * * * *

Lex pulled his Harley into the garage and walked up the back stairs into the main house. For the first time since he'd left earlier that day, he felt relaxed. Their home was one he'd designed to serve as a refuge from Pack business. The Pack did not come to their big wooden home in the woods. There was a Pack house in town where Lex and Cade spent several nights a week but this house was theirs and theirs alone. They'd watched Pack business take over every part of their father's life and eat at their parents' marriage. Neither Cade nor Lex wanted to make that same mistake.

Lex walked down the grand hallway and heard his brother, the Alpha of the Pack, clicking on the keyboard, working as usual. He walked into the home office that looked out over the lake and flopped onto the couch. "Hey."

"Hey, yourself. Did you find him?" Cade spun in his chair to look at his brother.

Lex sighed. "No. But I met his sister."

Cade raised a brow. "Oh yeah? And? I'm guessing you charmed her into bed and she told you where he was?"

Lex barked a laugh. "Try again. She fucking pointed a shotgun at my balls and told me to get lost."

Cade looked at him wide eyed and then burst out laughing. "No shit?"

"She looks like a librarian. Comes to the door in some prim and proper outfit, hair so tightly bound up she probably got a headache, and gives me the evil eye. Mouth puckered up like she'd been sucking lemons. The chick has Sunday school teacher written all over her.

"First she poked me in the chest! Then she told me that Rey showed up at her place—said he was being threatened by the Pack who wanted to kill him, grabbed some cash and took off. Then she told me to get out of there or she'd shoot me. I look down and she's got a shotgun planted in my crotch and the meanest look I've ever seen on a human on her face. She called me wolf boy, slammed the door in my face. Oh! And flipped me off when I was driving away," Lex said, unable to keep the admiration out of his voice.

Cade wiped a tear of mirth from his eye. "The most feared wolf in North America and a Sunday school teacher got the jump on you? Damn, I wish I could have seen it with my own eyes. You must be slipping, Lex. Clearly getting shot at and running after Rogue wolves isn't enough to keep your edge." He put his hand to his chin and pretended to think carefully. "Perhaps this woman should be our new Enforcer. Should we ask her, Lex? You can teach her kids and she can handle the firearms and take down the bad guys."

Lex shot his brother a dirty look. "Make fun while you can, dickweed. I'm telling you, despite her general level of homeliness and uptightness, she was fierce. It's kinda admirable."

"Admirable? And she's related to Rey? How come he's such a weasel then?"

"There's a messed up weasel in every family. Look at you." Lex smirked at his brother as he heaved himself off the couch and headed down the hall to the kitchen. He bent to grab a beer from the fridge and tossed one to Cade.

"Ha ha, very funny. Call me Alpha when you say that," Cade growled. "What's your plan, then, oh scary Enforcer?" Cade asked, tossing the beer cap into the recycling and leaning back against the wall.

Shoving past Cade, Lex moved to sit down at the table. "We watch the sister. You know Rey will need help. He's going to screw up sooner or later. Hell, she admitted that she'd cleaned up after him his whole life. When he comes to her, we'll grab him." Lex took a sip of the beer and shrugged his shoulders. "We have to find out what he saw."

"Well, we'd better hope we get to him before the Rogues do," Cade said.

"For his sake and ours. We have to find out what's going on. Until we do, no one can be trusted, and you can't run a Pack that way."

* * * * *

The next morning, as Nina walked to her car, she noticed the steel-gray Mercedes parked across the street. Upon closer examination, she saw Lex Warden sitting inside and sighed — partly in annoyance and partly at the picture he made there. He looked cool and dangerous and undeniably sexy with his carnal lips curled up at the corner into a smug smile. Pushing her attraction down as far as she could, she pulled out of her driveway and drove to work. He made no bones about following her and did so openly, probably to rattle her a bit. It didn't matter. She'd kept her cool under much scarier circumstances than some guy watching her. As long as Gabriel listened to her advice and had hightailed it out of town and kept his head low, everything would be all right.

She snorted to herself at that. Of course he wouldn't. He'd mess up because it was simply part of his nature. No, she could only hope when it did happen that it wasn't too catastrophic and that she got to him before the bad guys did.

With a sigh, she pulled into her space behind the florist shop and went inside to begin to prepare for the day. This was her realm. She'd built this business from the ground up and it was totally hers. Hers to make or break, and damn it, she'd made it through a heck of a lot of hard work and sixteen-hour days.

On her way through to the employee kitchen she took the place in, loving the little details. The antique pots and containers she picked up in little shops and garage and estate sales. The potted plants and lush greenery that made the shop seem like an oasis in the middle of a metropolitan area. The stained glass panes that she'd found last year were hung in the high windows and now morning light jeweled through them and across the floor and walls.

Smiling with satisfaction, she put her lunch into the fridge and grabbed a cup of coffee that was fresh and waiting for her, and her day officially began. Checking in with her assistant, she made sure that the wholesaler had made the early morning delivery and that everything had arrived as ordered.

Folding the doors back, she placed pretty buckets and basins of flowers directly outside of the shop, watered the hanging plants and went back inside. She made it a point to ignore Lex, who was now leaning against his car, drinking a coffee. She fell into her daily rhythm—she loved her shop, loved flowers and plants, and taking care of the daily minutiae of it all pulled her into a sort of Zen state.

Well, she'd be lying if she said she could ignore him entirely. He made quite a sight—long, muscular body lounging against that sexy car. His thighs strained the jeans he had on and all of that gorgeous hair was tied back at the nape of his neck. His large hands cradled a cup of coffee and she imagined what they'd feel like on her body. His designer sunglasses hid those beautiful green eyes but she knew his eyes followed her every move. His casual pose did not fool her, he was tight and alert and ready for anything.

Lex watched her as she moved about her small florist shop. She had an innate grace about her. He liked watching the way she put the arrangements together so beautifully, like it was second nature to her. She had an eye for beauty and apparently quite the green thumb. She chatted with customers and the employees and people seemed to really like her as they stopped into the shop just to say hello or to buy flowers. He hid a smile when he watched her run out to the mail carrier and tuck a bird of paradise into his bag. There was no trace of the poker-faced uptight spinster of the night before, except for those moments when she looked up and saw him—then it returned and her entire body stiffened. He wanted to grin at her when she did that. Her ire amused him. *She* amused him, and surprised him too. She was a lot tougher than she looked to stand there and act as if it were no big deal that a six-and-a-half-foot-tall werewolf was watching her every move.

He made his business calls from his cell phone as he watched her take lunch while working. He'd grown up in a family business, knew what it meant to work so hard you ate your lunch standing up and in a hurry. She seemed to be doing pretty well for herself if the traffic was any indicator. She'd had a steady flow of customers all day long and she seemed to know ninety percent of them personally.

* * * * *

At four, Brad came in and moved in and tried to drop a brief kiss on her lips. She stiffened and turned her head but as usual, he didn't catch that. "Nina, there's a guy across the street, he's been there all day. I think he's watching you."

Nina smiled at him as she stepped out of his reach. Brad Logan was the owner of the bookstore next door to the flower shop and he'd been pestering her to go out with him for months. He was actually quite good looking and Nina had no idea why he was interested in her, or rather, the public Nina anyway. She liked him well enough but he just didn't give her the spark of interest that would lead her to letting him into her closely guarded personal life. It had been awfully long though, since she'd let anyone inside. She found herself yearning to be close to someone she didn't have to save, protect or bail out of trouble. Someone who was an equal, a partner.

"I know. It's nothing," she assured him.

Brad looked at Lex again. "Who is he? Do you want me to go and talk to him?" Brad asked her, still concerned.

"He's an associate of my brother's. Everything's all right, Brad. Thanks for your concern though, I appreciate it."

"Why don't you let me escort you to your car when you close up? We could go out to dinner afterward."

"Not tonight, Brad. I have plans, but thanks. I'll be fine, he won't hurt me," she assured him and after a few minutes more of chatting, he went back next door.

Lex watched the scene with annoyed interest. His glittering green eyes narrowed behind the sunglasses he had on as he watched the human man touch her arm. Didn't he see that she wasn't interested? Lex felt an irrational desire to punch the guy out. "Stupid goatee," he snarled to himself.

It was dark when she locked up and walked out to her car. He could see her roll her eyes at his presence and he gave her a wolfish grin in return. He heard her annoyed exhalation and chuckled as he followed her to the grocery store.

At the market, she shopped and tried to ignore his presence. Of course she failed when he simply walked behind her as she pushed her cart. In the produce aisle he took a cantaloupe out of her hands and picked up another and handed it to her.

She had a look of disbelief on her face and he wanted to laugh. Instead he said, "That one wasn't any good. I have a great sense of smell, you know. The one you have now is ripe and sweet. I promise."

She closed her eyes for a moment and it looked like she was praying for patience. He bit the inside of his cheek to keep from laughing. With a barely leashed snarl of her own, she pushed her cart around him and kept shopping, but she didn't put the cantaloupe back.

She paid and loaded her groceries into the trunk and he followed her back to her house, where he pulled up into the driveway behind her.

She spun, hands on her hips and sparks in her eyes. "What are you doing? I told you, Gabriel is not here!" she said through clenched teeth as he approached her car, where she'd been pulling out bags of groceries.

"I was going to help you carry your groceries in. That way you won't have to make two trips."

She sighed and waved at the bags. If he wanted to do some grunt work to make up for her extreme annoyance with him that was fine with her. She unlocked her door and motioned him toward the kitchen. She told herself that she was only doing it to watch his spectacular ass but she admitted to herself that she liked him. Even if he was a pain in the ass.

"Go ahead, get a good look and get the hell out," she said as he set the bags down on the counter. She began to open up cabinets and the fridge and put the food away, acting as if he wasn't even there.

"What? No thank you for hauling your groceries?" he teased.

She looked back over her shoulder and raised an eyebrow at him. "Make it quick, wolf boy. I may just change my mind and toss you out."

It was his turn to give her a raised brow. He was a werewolf in his prime. The most feared Enforcer in North America. Heck, people were downright scared of him. He stood there, all muscle and sinew—there was no way that she could budge him, even if she took a running leap.

"Smirk all you want, I've warned you," she said in a nearly sing-song voice that made him bark out a laugh. She caught him off guard, he liked that.

He was a damned good tracker, it was one of the reasons why he was an excellent Enforcer. He always found his man. Focusing on Rey's scent, he moved through the house, but the only place that he could get it strongly was in the kitchen near the back door. He continued through the house, through the small living room with the cozy overstuffed couch and side chairs. Pausing, he looked at her living space. It was simple but extremely warm and welcoming. She had great built-in bookshelves. The decoration was at a minimum but what she did have up—some really nice black-and-white prints—lent a touch of class to the place. He peeked into the spare bedroom, which looked like an office, and then went across the hall and into her bedroom.

Standing in the doorway, he groaned as his senses took in the intimate space. It was soft and feminine. The bed was covered a pale blue fluffy comforter, and pillows in various shades of complementary blue were scattered all over the room. The headboard was white wrought iron and there was a stack of books at least three feet high next to the bed. He took a step inside and her scent hit him right in the balls. He closed his eyes as he breathed her in, the soft vanilla scent of her soap, a bit of citrus from her shampoo. No perfume. Her elemental scent was everywhere and it made the wolf within want to go and roll in her blankets, to coat himself in it.

He shook his head to clear it. Oh no, it was not going to go down this way. He needed to get laid and not by some uptight spinster either. He made a mental note to seek out some company when he went to the Pack house later.

"So? Satisfied Gabriel isn't hiding in my closet or under my bed?" she asked as she walked down the hallway toward him.

Surprised by her voice, he jumped and turned. "Look, lady, it's really important that I talk to him." His annoyance at being so affected by her scent rang through his voice.

She noticed and put her arms over her chest and narrowed her big brown eyes at him. "Stop calling me that," she snapped.

"So you do have emotions under that hard shell." He grinned.

She shook her head in disgust. "Look, wolf boy, why do you want to talk to Gabriel? What have you people, er, wolves, done to him?"

He smirked at her. "Wolf boy? You object to lady and then call me wolf boy?"

"I never said I wasn't a hypocrite. But this is my house so I get the privilege and you don't. Now, what do you want with Gabriel?"

He sighed and ran a hand through his thick, silky-looking hair, pulling it loose from the thong at his neck. It spilled over his hands and past his shoulders like liquid silk. She could smell his cologne and beneath it, his maleness. He smelled hot and hard—like sex on legs. He smelled dangerous and capable of violence and she had to take a deep breath through her mouth to stop shaking. There was such a ravenous hunger for him that it shocked her into silence for a few moments.

"He might have seen something he wasn't supposed to have seen. I need to know if he did. His life is at stake here. Did he say anything to you?"

She snorted. Of course he saw something he shouldn't have. Studboy the wolf man wouldn't be harassing her if he hadn't. "His life is always at stake. It has been since before one of you assholes gave him the virus. He has no common sense, no ability to function on his own. When you...people, took him into your gang, Pack—whatever—you became, for better or for worse, his parents, his government, and now whatever the hell he got into has chased him off. He didn't tell me anything, he took the only money I had in cash here and left in a big hurry."

He scrubbed his face with his hands. "We are *not* a gang!" Taking a deep breath, he wanted to groan as her scent crawled into his body. He had to get out of there, and right away. Before he jumped on her. "If he calls, will you tell him to contact me? He's got my cell phone number. It's urgent. I truly don't want to hurt your brother but there are those who will if he saw something he wasn't supposed to. If he can tell me what he saw, I can use that to punish the guilty parties and protect him at the same time."

"If he calls me, which god knows if he will—I've only heard from him rarely over the last several years—I'll tell him what you said. I'll also advise him to go to the cops. I doubt he'll listen to either suggestion."

"The cops can't help him." His senses honed in on her. There was something that had changed. She now had a harder edge than he'd seen before. A less polished veneer, and it wasn't the bird she flipped or the shotgun—her eyes were hard, even behind the glasses.

She gave a very tired sigh. "No one can, Mr. Warden. Now please go."

He nodded and walked out into the night and drove away.

* * * * *

Sitting in the rare April sunshine, Nina ate her sandwich. She tipped her face up to grab all the natural light she could before having to get back to work.

"Heard from Rey?"

She sighed heavily, opened her eyes and took in the gloriously male thighs that belonged to her shadow and nemesis, Lex Warden. Damn but the man was delicious.

"I thought we went over this, wolf boy. He hasn't contacted me. I told you that I'd relay your message if he did.

25

Anyway, let's not pretend that you and your furry minions haven't been watching my every move for the last two weeks."

For a spinster she really was funny. For the hundredth time he found himself wanting to take her hair out of that ruthlessly tight bun and toss the glasses away. Wanting to know what she was like beneath the uptight veneer. Truth was, spinster or not, he liked her. More than that, he admired her. Okay, so it was more than that, he had to admit that he was sweet on her. Each time he saw her, watched her, caught her scent on the breeze, he wanted her a bit more.

"Furry minions?" He grinned at her, gave her his teeth and all of his charm and stilled for a moment. He scented her arousal. Her body warmed and he smelled her pussy. It couldn't be. She hated him.

She stood up, tossed her garbage into the bin and moved past him, back into her shop. "I'd say you'd be the first to know if he contacts me, but I'd be lying. Have a good day, wolf boy," she tossed over her shoulder as she went back inside.

He stood there, stunned, for a few minutes and then growled as he stomped away, frustrated that his body wanted a woman like her instead of the very willing females at the Pack house.

* * * * *

A week later, Nina awoke from a deep sleep and sat straight up with a gasp. Someone was in her house. She grabbed her shotgun and crept out into the hallway and nearly shot her brother as he rummaged through her fridge.

"Jesus! Gabriel, I almost shot you," she said in a hiss, hand over her frantic heart.

He turned to her and grinned. "Sorry, I was starving."

"What in hell are you doing here? Gabriel, your Pack has been looking for you. Lex Warden has been here several times and he's been following me. And when he isn't stuck to my ass, one of his men, people, wolves..." She shook her head in confusion. "Anyway, I'm constantly being watched. He says he wants to help you. That others want to kill you. It's time for you to tell me exactly what you saw."

His grin faded and he took his food to the table and sat down heavily. "Nina, there's some bad shit going on. I told you that I saw them kill my bud Tommie. It's one of the Pack hierarchy, I know that much for sure. He was talking to them one minute and the next he was on the sidewalk in a pool of blood. I got the hell out of there but I'm pretty sure they saw me."

"Ya think?" she said sarcastically. "You saw a murder, Gabriel. Damn it, listen to me for once and go to the cops!"

"Oh how naïve can you be? Come on, Nina! You may be living the straight life now but you know that we can't go to them. One run of my record and they wouldn't believe a damned thing I say. And you want them back in your life?"

"Of course I don't! But that doesn't change what happened. You saw a murder." She broke off, frustrated with him, with the situation. Struggling for calm, she took a deep breath. "Why, Gabe? Why did they kill your friend?"

"I don't know!" He threw his hands up in frustration. "He said he was on some business for Cade and had to talk to someone, someone big. He told me to keep it quiet. He'd met with these guys before but I could tell he was really nervous."

"Do you know anything other than that? Anything that we can use to keep you alive? Find out who killed your friend and why?"

Gabriel nodded earnestly. "Yes! He had a laptop, left it in the car. It's in our locker at the bus station. I don't know how to get the information off it."

She sighed, knowing what was next. "Why didn't you tell me this before?" She was so sick of his convoluted thinking. This had been going on for weeks and he had a big clue just sitting around? She took a calming breath. "Cade is Lex's brother right? The Alpha? Can you trust him? If you can't go to the cops, he's the nearest thing isn't he?"

"I don't know how high this thing goes. Both Wardens seem to be pretty good guys, but the shooter is in the top Pack ranks, or he is according to what Tommie told me before he got capped. Until we see what's on that laptop, how can I know who to trust?"

"Did you turn it on?"

He nodded. "Looks like some heavy security protocol shit, though. I left it alone, figured your expertise was needed."

She sighed but couldn't deny the thrill she felt. It had been a very long time since she'd done anything exciting or shady. "Let me get dressed and we'll go." She turned and walked into her bedroom and pulled on some jeans and a sweatshirt, gathering her hair into a tight ponytail and grabbing the glasses.

"What, no ugly clothes?" he cracked as she came back into the kitchen.

"It's in between my disguise and my normal look. Not wearing a disguise is as good as wearing one. Everyone connected with your Pack knows me as the uptight matron with the granny clothes so the jeans and sweatshirt might fool them, but if my neighbors saw, they'd still see the hair pulled back and the glasses."

"You're so smart, why can't I ever think of stuff like that?"

She would have said something sarcastic but he looked so forlorn that she held back and kissed the top of his head instead. "I'm here for you, Gabriel. We'll get through this together, like always. Let's go." She grabbed her own laptop and gear.

She knew she was being watched so they quietly went into the garage. Needing to avoid being seen, Gabriel crouched down on the floorboard in the backseat until they got out of the immediate area.

* * * * *

Her skills were rusty, but being dodgy was like riding a bike. She laughed to herself as she looked in the rearview mirror, seeing it empty. She had a feeling that Lex Warden wouldn't be so easy to shake the next time. She'd taken advantage of the fact that she knew he'd underestimate her but she also knew he wouldn't do it twice. Lex Warden was damned good at his job. She admired that about him. It was sexy.

She pulled into the parking lot at the bus station in downtown Seattle and turned to Gabriel. "Stay in the car. We don't know how many people are looking for you but it's wise to keep your head down. I'll be back in a few."

Leaving Gabriel in the car, she went into the building and did a good solid meander around making sure she wasn't being followed and finally went to the lockers. She pulled out two keys, one for her locker and one for the one she shared with Gabriel. Out of her locker she pulled out what she termed her running kit. A gym bag with clothes, a cell phone, cash, a laptop and several electronic toys — the tools she'd need to get out of town quickly and to help her set up somewhere else. It had sat there for five years. She'd added to it over that time, extra money, a new toy here and there — it made her feel safe, knowing she had a back door out of trouble. She planned to give most of it to Gabriel and send him far, far away when she got him back to his motel room.

She opened up the other locker, Gabriel's locker, and saw the laptop case. Grabbing it, she slammed the doors closed, walked out of the bus station and got back into her car.

"Got it. Let's go back to your motel and see what we can find. I don't want to take you back to my house, not with Warden skulking around."

Gabriel nodded. "I don't think he's dirty, Nina. He's a pretty stand-up guy. Maybe I should take this to him," he said worriedly. "I'm tired of hiding."

It had only been a few weeks. Her stomach sank. If he couldn't deal with a little less than a month on the run, how could he survive in the long term? She had to figure out who was behind this shooting so that she could use the information to buy Gabriel's freedom. There was no other way.

"Let's see what's on this machine before we do anything, okay?" She spared a quick glance his way, the street lights casting an orange glow, flickering over his face as they passed by. He wasn't thirty yet and already he had lived a hard life. Poverty, abuse, lawlessness, neglect—that combined with too much alcohol had given his once sweet face a hardened edge.

She sighed, not for the first time, grieving for what might have been for Gabriel but quickly put it away. She couldn't afford to wallow, certainly not now.

They turned into the parking lot of a seedy motel near the airport and she pulled in to the back, out of sight of the street. She bit back her instinctual lecture on his choice of motel. The place was in town and within ten miles of the Pack house, but lectures would be pointless.

They went into the room and she put her stuff down. Looking down, she realized she'd left the kit in the car. She headed back to the door. "I'll be right back," she called out as she left the room.

"Need help?" Gabriel called out as he followed her outside, wearing a sweet smile. In that face was the Gabe of her childhood, the sweet little boy with nothing to hide, a loving and happy kid who had a family that took care of him. Her heart constricted in her chest at the memories of that very long ago Gabriel Reyes and mourned his loss.

She bent to unlock the car and felt the prickle on the back of her neck. *Trouble.* Time slowed as she spun around just as they were jumped. Four very large men, wolves she'd be willing to bet, rushed at them from out of the darkness.

Gabriel snarled as his wolf began to surface in reaction to the threat. He called out to Nina to run, to get out of there, as two of the wolves grabbed him. "Get off my sister!" he said in a growl as he attempted to fight free.

One of the wolves had Nina's ponytail in a tight grip and yanked her backwards. Facing her brother as she struggled, Nina watched, horrified, as one man put a gun to her brother's head and pulled the trigger. A cry of gut-wrenching grief tore from her as he crumpled to the ground. Sound, time, movement rushed back at her at super speed. She screamed as loudly as she could and delivered an elbow to the jaw of one of her attackers. She spun and gave a roundhouse kick to the solar plexus of the other and a good, solid right hook back to the first one. Both hit the deck and she turned back to where the man with the gun was, expecting to be shot at any moment.

But the shooter suddenly crumpled. She looked up and saw Lex standing there, fury on his face and blood on claws that slowly morphed back into a human hand.

She lost her footing for a moment and then scrambled to her feet. Ruthlessly, she tried to think, compartmentalized as best she could. She didn't have the time to fall apart! Forcing her thoughts away from how Gabriel's eyes had blanked, losing their life after he'd been shot, she attempted to focus. But the slice of reality cut through her, she was alone in the world.

No! She would not let that stop her now. Nina Reyes was not a quitter. She would see this through until she found out who killed her brother. There was time to fall apart later, but for now she was in a bad place. Shaking her head clear, she heard men around her, saw people moving bodies quickly.

Lex looked at her long and hard and she backed up a step, glancing right and left, looking for an avenue of escape. She was pale. He could see her pulse beating erratically in her throat. Her hair was partially out of the ponytail she had it in, her glasses were on the ground and he bent to pick them up. Surreptitiously, he wiped off the blood spatters.

"Don't even think about it, Nina. My brother is right behind you. There's nowhere to go." He looked her over carefully. "Are you all right?" he asked in low, soothing tones. He handed her glasses to her. "Here, you probably need these."

"Get. Out. Of. My. Way." She enunciated each word very carefully. Her lip was swelling where one of the thugs had hit her and she tasted blood. She also had a very sore arm where one of them had yanked on her. She tried to rotate her shoulder without bringing attention to it but of course both werewolves noticed it.

"Do you know who shot him?" The other werewolf came to stand next to her.

"Obviously one of you people. He said it was one of you. That he didn't know if he could trust you. Now let me go or I'm going to scream my head off. It might be close to midnight but there are plenty of people around." She said it in a flat voice but it was backed up by steel.

Cade held back a grim smile of approval. She'd just lost her brother and didn't trust them at all. Despite that, he liked her style. She wasn't going to give in without a fight. He gave a long look at the legs and ass encased in the jeans she was wearing. She was certainly no spinster librarian that he could tell. Sure, her hair was back tight from her face and her glasses were thick but the way she looked in jeans wasn't something to overlook. Then again, he had a thing for librarians—he thought they were all sexy.

"We aren't going to hurt you. We're on your side." Cade was straightforward, he saw no need to speak softly. She wanted to know what was going on.

She shook her head. "You're here, aren't you? With them. You expect me to believe it's just a coincidence that you showed up at the same time as werewolf hit men?"

Lex gave a frustrated sigh. "We aren't here *with* them. We came here looking for you and saved you from them." He jammed his hands into his pockets, the failure of letting one of his own die washing over him. Two of his people in a month, the bitter taste of it was metallic in his mouth. "Look, we suspect that some of our own are up to something but we don't know what. One of the wolves we had looking into it is the one who got killed."

"Oh, you're a fucking genius. I can see now why you're in charge," she said sarcastically, rolling her eyes at him. "If you aren't with them, how did you find me?" she asked, suspicious.

Lex leaned over and pulled a tracking device from the wheel well of her car. She cursed quietly.

"Why don't you come back to the house with us? We can protect you. You can't go home. Your house," he hesitated, "your house was on fire when I doubled back after you ditched me." He got a sour look. "I'm sorry, I couldn't do anything. The fire department was pulling down the street when I drove past. By the time I got there it was already too far gone. They used an accelerant of some type, I could smell it. The guy who shot Rey, he has the scent on him."

Suddenly she surfaced, remembering what had just happened. Spinning, she saw her brother's body was gone. She surged forward and grabbed Cade's shirt and heard growling in the background.

"Stand down," Cade growled back at the men who'd stood forward to protect him. He gently but firmly took her upper arms and looked into her eyes.

"You have Gabriel's body? Where is he?" she demanded.

He slid his hands gently down her arms and took hers, reading the grief in her eyes. "One of my lieutenants has him.

We needed to take him away from the scene. We can't deal with the cops until we figure out what's going on. We'll give him a proper burial, I promise," he said softly. "He was one of ours, he'll be buried as Pack."

Lex felt the need to rip his brother away from Nina. To shield her from all other men. Damn it, but he had to admit it to himself before he went crazy. He'd been feeling that way since that day in her shop when the other man had touched her, kissed her, and it had only worsened when he smelled her room. He'd stopped by the Pack house several times, meaning to find some female company — god knew that there were plenty of females who wanted to share his bed. He'd really tried but not a single one appealed to him.

He knew that if he got close enough to bury his face in her neck, scenting the glands there, that he'd find the scent of his woman. He didn't want to, he liked being a bachelor, and yet, he yearned for her with every fiber of his being. His cock hardened in response to the thought. Pheromones didn't lie, not to his wolf. She was the one for him. Her genes called out to his, she was his ideal mate, end of story. He sighed, resigned to it at last.

He stepped forward and put himself between her and Cade. "Let's get out of the open. You're bleeding, I can smell it. We need to get that taken care of. Which one was Rey's room?" Lex asked gently.

She pointed listlessly and Lex put an arm about her shoulders and led her inside. Taking care of her like that, protecting her, felt so right that he realized just how wrong everything had been until that moment. Lex sat her down on the bed and stood back, frowning as he took in the split lip and the beginnings of a bruise on her neck. If he hadn't already killed the wolf who'd done that to her, he'd be out there right now tracking him. Lex's wolf paced inside of his body, anxious to lash out and hurt anyone who'd harm his woman.

He got a wet washcloth and she held still while he dabbed at her lip, looking carefully at the marks on her neck to be sure the skin hadn't broken. Satisfied, he moved to toss the cloth into the sink while Cade rustled around.

Nina took the glass of water Cade offered, grateful to have something to do with her hands. Drinking, she closed her eyes, trying to hold herself together. She had to fight against the numbness that threatened. At the same time, all she wanted to do was bury her face in Lex Warden's neck and hold on until he made everything all right. That freaked her out almost as much as losing Gabriel did.

Oh, Gabriel, it shouldn't have been this way! All her life she'd been the strong one. She'd taken care of Gabriel from the time she was twelve and he was eight. Their parents had died in a hotel fire and they'd gone to live with distant cousins who couldn't have cared less about either one of them. They'd let Gabriel run wild and he'd gotten in with the wrong crowd. Soon they'd gotten kicked out of the house and Nina'd had to hustle to make sure they were able to survive. She learned and ran all manner of street cons to pay rent while she made sure that Gabriel got an education.

She discovered hacking accidentally while taking a computer programming class in the local adult education program. She'd had an innate skill and knowledge of computers and programming, and started hacking for fun when she was working for a woman who'd helped them out and taken them in. She'd realized that she could make money more safely and quickly through hacking than out on the street dodging not only the cops, but the pimps and drug dealers too.

Over the next several years she'd become one of the best. She developed a reputation for quick, clean jobs that were high risk. She had to be good, Gabriel was constantly in trouble and she had to bail him out. They'd moved dozens of times, staying one step ahead of the law. She'd promised Gabriel the day they walked away from their cousins' house that there was no way she was going to let the authorities break them up.

Her reputation grew to be legendary, as such things go anyway. Shiningstarr was a name revered by fellow hackers and tech geeks. It was also a name that attracted the attention of the authorities.

As her skills grew, she got to the point where she worked on spec for a few people and made enough money to save. Nina wasn't greedy but she'd wanted money in case she needed it. She took the jobs until it became too risky to continue. She also got tired of being on the run and feeling guilty over breaking the law. When the offer came for a big and very risky job, she took it. It was a big payoff, enough to give them both a new start, and she'd promised herself and Gabriel that she'd go straight when it was over.

She'd taken her money and she and Gabriel had fled Ohio for Seattle. It had been too big a risk to choose a path that had anything to do with computers. She had gotten close to getting caught a few times and hadn't wanted to chance it. She'd been so tired of running and living on the margins. She'd wanted a normal life, a real job. Security. So she'd enrolled in a floral design program and some business courses at the local community college and then she'd taken part of her nest egg and opened her florist shop. She discovered that working with flowers and plants was something she not only loved, but was good at. It wasn't the big money game that hacking had been but it wasn't illegal either. She could relax finally, for the first time since she'd been twelve. While she tinkered around as a hobby with her computer skills, she'd ruthlessly tamped down any use of the internet for anything other than her business.

Things had been going really well until Gabriel had gotten infected with the lycanthropy virus during a bar fight. He'd hit on some guy's girlfriend and the guy, being a total jerk, had infected him on purpose in the fight. Gabriel very nearly didn't make it then. Instead of pressing charges against the wolf for intentionally infecting him, instead of turning his life around, he joined the local Pack and became a runner, a man-of-all-work essentially, and had dropped off her radar.

She was so tired. She'd given up running years ago. She had built a life for herself in Seattle. She had friends and her business. Granted she hadn't had a date in four years, but there never seemed to be much time for that anyway.

Her house was gone, her stuff was gone and her brother, the last bit of family she had any feelings for, was gone. She wasn't going to leave town, damn it! Her business was her life—the only thing she had left. She wasn't going to allow some punks to run her off.

"You really can trust me," Lex said, pushing his brother out of the way. "Me and Cade. If we were planning on hurting you, we could have done so already. Not that you're not a tough customer, I know you can handle yourself," he added quickly when her eyes narrowed.

"I'm going to have one of my men take your car and hide it. You can come back with us, our house is safe."

"Of course it isn't safe! Someone high up in your Pack hierarchy is the one who shot what's-his-face," she hissed, leaning back from Lex Warden's body. She had this awful compulsion to rub her cheek along his chest, to tug his bottom lip between her teeth. His cologne was obviously doing something to her.

"Did Rey tell you who, Nina?" Cade asked.

She shook her head. "He said it was someone big, that what's-his-face told him it was someone high up. Gabriel didn't see anyone's face, though. God, they killed him for no reason! He didn't know anything."

"Damn it! I told you, Cade," Lex said, and as he moved she saw the big gun in the shoulder holster and she stiffened.

Oblivious, Lex brushed his hands through his hair again. It made Nina's body tighten just to watch. Oh jeez, perfect timing to get horny, right after your brother is killed and you might be next. Truthfully, she knew that Lex was right. If they'd wanted to hurt her, they could have quite easily. But damn it, she didn't know up from down and she felt totally off balance.

"I just didn't want to believe it. Thank god you pulled all clearance but yours and mine." Cade turned back to Nina. "No one is allowed at the house but me and Lex and my personal guard. All of us are Wardens, absolutely trustworthy. We have a Pack house here in town for everyone else, but my house is a safe haven. You'll be safe there. We've got to get out of here in case reinforcements show up."

Safe from the killer sure—but not from Lex. And Nina had a feeling that Lex Warden posed a way bigger threat to her than any scary werewolves who wanted to kill her. Still, she wasn't going to let go until the guy who killed her brother was taken care of.

She took a deep breath and tried to relax. "Okay, for now. But I need to deal with the cops about my house and call my assistant to deal with my business."

Lex nodded and stifled a predatory smile as they grabbed her stuff from the room and her car and headed to Lex's Mercedes. When he got into the back with her and let his brother drive, Cade raised a brow in the rearview mirror but said nothing.

"What were you doing here, anyway?" Lex asked her as they drove away, heading east.

"I was going to check out the laptop my brother said belonged to the guy who got shot."

Lex looked at her sharply for a moment and then down at the computer case she held. "You what? I've been watching you for weeks now. Why didn't you tell me that?"

"I just did."

He barely held his annoyance in check. Mate or not, the woman was a pain in the ass. "Earlier," he ground out through clenched teeth.

"I had to be sure I could trust you." She wasn't going to apologize!

"What's on it?"

"Dunno. Gabriel said that he couldn't get in. He came to me for help." Her voice broke on the last word and Lex reached out, took her hand in his own and squeezed it. He'd been angry at her for not telling them about the laptop, but seeing how upset she was pushed all of that aside. He just wanted to make it better for her.

"How? How were you going to help? Do you know a computer expert?" Cade asked and she chuckled wearily.

"I *am* a computer expert. I've never met a program that can lock me out. It may take me a while to get in, but I will. I haven't even booted it yet." She shrugged as she looked out the window at nothing. "I didn't want to open it up until I got somewhere where I could hook it up to my own laptop with some security protocols. Gabriel should have been smart enough not to trigger any defensive viral programs but we'll see. I went out to my car to get my kit, I forgot it. Gabriel came out to see if I needed help..." she choked out, unable to say anything else.

Lex didn't say much more as they continued east. He ached to make it better for her, to pull her into the shelter of his body and hold her. But he knew she wasn't ready for that so he kept her hand in his own and pushed his overwhelming desire for her to the side—for the time being.

* * * * *

Cade pulled into a long drive. Midway a set of large iron gates stood closed. He slid the car to a stop next to a keypad and rolled the window down. He quickly keyed in a code as Nina cast a quick, assessing glance at the setup.

"What do you think?" Lex asked, seeing her curious look. "If you're a computer expert, I take it you know about security too?"

She leaned over him to get a better look through the window. She gave a low whistle. "State of the art. I could hack it, even remotely, but it would take me a while. While I'm here, remind me to check your security system."

"I'd appreciate that," Lex said.

Nodding absently, she only barely held back a gasp when they came around the bend and the house came into view.

Impressive was the first word that came to mind. Fronted entirely by glass, it loomed out of the hillside and undoubtedly had some prime views. It was one of those places that graced the cover of architectural and design magazines. This was no cookie-cutter house—someone with a great mind and a lot of talent had created it. The cleverly landscaped gardens that surrounded it gave a sense of wildness and burst with a riot of color. There were trees everywhere and hanging baskets, containers that were overflowing with flowers and plants, and she could see several water features as well. The house was an oasis.

They pulled into a garage with three other bays. There was a Mercedes and two motorcycles, including the Harley that she'd seen Lex ride on multiple occasions. Lex grabbed her stuff but she kept her kit. He sighed and then shrugged, turning to lead her inside.

When they came into the lower level of the house from the garage she made a low sound of pleased surprise. The view through the big glass walls was of the entire valley below and the forests all around.

A spiral stair led from the lower hallway upward to what looked to be the main living level. Sleek modern furniture decorated a large living room bisected by a gigantic fireplace that created a wall into an entertainment room with state-of-the-art electronics.

They headed up another staircase—this one wider—to the next floor. Lex led her down a long hallway with skylights. She could see the night stars winking above her as they walked. He opened a door almost at the end and waved her inside, dropping her bags as she passed.

He gestured at the room, which was large and airy and had a balcony with French doors that overlooked the gardens at the side of the house. There was a large bed with white wrought ironwork and saffron-and-red-accented linens. "I'm going to put you here in the guestroom. It's got its own bathroom and fireplace. We have a higher body core temperature and so the house is colder than one where a human would live. It's a gas fireplace and it heats the room well. Are you hungry?" He snapped his mouth closed as he realized with horror that he was actually babbling. This human woman had reduced him to a blathering mess. He had to fuck her and claim her as soon as possible.

She looked around the room, sighing tiredly. She was barely holding back the tears and desperately needed to be alone before she lost it in front of him. "It's nearly two, I'm exhausted. I have to call my staff to tell them to open the shop tomorrow. I can't think about food or that computer right now..." Her sentence trailed off as he held her gaze.

Sneaking a quick look at the bag that held her laptop, he held off pressuring her. Dark circles smudged beneath her eyes, lines of grief etched around her mouth. Unable to stop himself, he reached out, running the pad of his thumb over her bottom lip.

She closed her eyes, allowing him that brief contact. The warmth of his touch slid sinuously through her system and her nipples hardened. Alarmed again at how he affected her, she stepped back, clearing her throat. "Thank you for letting me stay here."

He let her avoid him. For the moment. "You're welcome here. You're *safe* here, I promise you. You know, it occurs to me you haven't told me your name."

"I'm Nina, but you must have known that from Gabriel or you wouldn't have known where I lived."

He gave a quiet chuckle. "Well yes, but we haven't been properly introduced. He talked about you all of the time—his big sister who was always helping him. He wanted to prove himself to you." He stopped speaking, his smile faltered when he watched more grief come into her eyes. "I am sorry for your loss, Nina. Rey loved you."

At least he didn't try saying what an important asset Gabriel was to them or any such lie. She nodded. "I really need to sleep," she said, trying not to plead. She needed some distance from Lex and she needed it before she did or said something stupid like jump on him as she cried, *please take off your pants and give me comfort with your cock.*

He cleared his throat and she snapped back to reality. "Hang on a sec." He sprinted down the hall and came back a few moments later.

Handing her a neatly folded stack of clothes he stood back, almost looking shy. "Here. They're going to be too big but it occurred to me that you may not have any clothes to sleep in. Please, call out if you need me. I'm only two doors down." He walked to the door and looked back at her one last time before leaving the room quietly.

She had two changes of clothes in the running kit but no night clothes, so she rooted through the clothes he'd brought and found a pajama top that smelled of him. On autopilot, she hugged it to her body as she padded into the bathroom that adjoined the bedroom.

The room was as large as her bedroom at home. A terrible pain sliced through her as she realized that she had no home anymore. Her books, her music, her clothing, it was as gone as Gabriel was. She'd bought her little bungalow two years before. She could have chosen something more expensive, she had some money left over from what she'd spent on the business, but she'd wanted to buy it free and clear without showing up on any radar. So she'd scrimped and saved and made it her own, planting her own garden and decorating it slowly but surely. She still had about three hundred thousand dollars in a Swiss account but she felt guilty about that money and left it there to be used only in an emergency.

She turned on the water and let it go very hot. The room filled with steam as her vision blurred. As she stepped into the glass enclosure the first racking sob tore through her and she stood there, face turned up to the water, letting the tears flow freely.

She felt so alone. She had no one left who was part of her, and that made her feel bereft. Adrift. At the same time, she couldn't deny the small part of her that felt freer now that she wasn't responsible for someone else. She wouldn't be cleaning up after Gabriel anymore. Of course that just made her feel guilty on top of alone and grief-stricken, and the tears came harder.

The water began to cool just as she had nothing left. Like a zombie, she got out and dried off, slipping into the shirt. It felt good against her skin—Lex's scent wrapped around her, giving her comfort. With a heavy sigh she pulled back the bedding and slid between the sheets. Her last thought was that she'd have to deal with the cops and her house first thing, and then she promptly passed out.

* * * * *

Down the hall, in the office outside of Cade's bedroom, Lex heard her turn on the shower and then his stomach clenched as he heard her sobs. He stood up and started to leave the room, to go to her and pull her into his arms. Cade put his hand out and barred the door.

"Where are you going?"

"She's hurting! I'm going to go to her."

Cade heard the anguish in his brother's voice and hid a smile. "Why? I thought you weren't interested in her," Cade said with mock casualness. "I think she's pretty exceptional. That roundhouse and the right hook? Wow. Anyway, you think she's a dried-up spinster, I'll go in and comfort her." He moved to leave the room.

Lex's hand shot out and grabbed his brother's shirt. "Stay away from her," he growled.

Cade laughed with delight. "I knew it!"

Lex rolled his eyes at his brother. "She's mine, Cade. Period."

Cade kept grinning and slapped Lex's back. Sobering, he said, "let her grieve, Lex. She's lost everything. Tomorrow morning is soon enough to pursue her. And she's going to give you such a hard time about it too. I can't wait." He rubbed his hands together in anticipation.

Chapter Two

ဢ

Carter Peterson paced, scrubbing his hands over his face. Stopping, he spun and glared at man standing before him, growling in frustration. "You didn't kill her? What the hell is wrong with you? She's a bloody human for goodness' sake!"

John Hendrix snorted in disgust. "We would have had her but the Enforcer and Alpha showed up with the guard. We took care of Gabriel Reyes, though. He can't say a freaking word now. For all we know, he didn't tell her a thing." The other werewolves in the room shifted uneasily as they watched the exchange.

Carter narrowed his eyes at the Rogue, lip curled in disgust. The Rogues were almost as bad as the damned humans. Disorganized, lazy. If he didn't have half a million dollars of debt to the mob hanging over his head, he'd have walked away from these wolves months ago.

"The operative phrase is that *we don't know!* What if Tommie told Rey and Rey told his sister? Huh? She tells the Wardens and The Enforcer shows up and rips my throat out. You need to figure out what the hell is going on, Hendrix! No more loose ends or this could all go sideways in record time. Kill the human and do it as soon as possible."

* * * * *

Lex woke up and got dressed. He spoke to his people and looked over their reports. As Enforcer for the Cascadia Clan, it was his job to oversee security. He was Cade's personal bodyguard, although his brother had a retinue of six guards who were on the property at all times. These guards were, every last one, Wardens. The Alpha of the Cascadia Clan had been a Warden for a hundred and fifty years and his family had held positions in top hierarchy for at least five hundred years. Theirs was an old and noble line.

Lex had been born to be an Enforcer. As second son and largest of all his siblings, he would be second-in-command and had been trained to fulfill that role from a very early age. Cade was the firstborn and as such, groomed to be alpha from birth. He was politically astute and charismatic, leading their Pack suited him. They had sisters as well, two of whom were in the personal guard. Cousins made up the rest of the retinue.

Lex Warden was feared and respected across all Clan territories. He was a badass and he wasn't afraid to admit it to himself. He not only had the natural abilities to serve as Enforcer, but had also received extensive training when he was an Army Ranger for eight years. It was rare that wolves messed with him and if and when they did, he crushed them without mercy.

He was also an architect and had designed the house that they lived in. While his biology and duty called him to be the Enforcer for the Cascadia Pack, his creativity led him to design. He enjoyed it and hoped to continue to grow his business. He'd done several homes on contract and a building in downtown Bellevue and he loved it. Loved the satisfaction of driving past one of the places that he'd created.

But for now his responsibility was to figure out just what was going on in the Pack and to claim the woman down the hall as his mate. If she were a wolf it would be relatively easy. She'd understand the attraction of their pheromones and would submit. But she was human, and in his experience human women never made anything easy.

He tucked his shirt in as he stalked down the hallway. As he neared her door he heard her muttering and the clacking of her typing. Giving a quick tap on the door, he opened it and froze as he caught sight of her.

Mouth gaping open, he took her in. She was sitting on one of the chairs, the laptop in her lap. Her bottom lip was caught between her teeth as she typed madly. She was also wearing only his pajama top. Impossibly, his cock hardened more until he actually winced in pain. Gone was the uptight matron, and in her place was a goddess.

Chocolate brown curls tumbled about her shoulders and arms, shiny and lustrous. Her eyes were a luminous brown, wide and fringed with thick black lashes. Her legs were long and athletic and the curve of her breasts was visible at the top of the pajama shirt she wore. Her skin was the color of milky coffee and looked silky and soft. He clenched his fists to keep from touching her but his eyes greedily soaked her in.

Hearing his strangled moan, she looked up, startled. Seeing him, she sent him a smile that made his insides warm. "Oh, good morning. I've called my staff and also the cops. I used my cell phone, said I was away from home and saw it on the news. I have to go in later today to talk about the fire. I hope to god they don't think I set my own house on fire. It's all so suspicious."

"I was thinking about that last night. We can say you were with me. Here. In my bed. All night." He had been thinking of it, of good alibis for her. But the bed thing came to him when he saw her sitting there like a luscious dessert.

Her pulse fluttered and she only barely leashed her gasp. "Uh, oh...yeah, er." Could she be any more incoherent? She took a deep breath. "Okay, yeah, that's probably a good idea."

"I'll come with you when you go. Since I'm your boyfriend and all." He said it like he was kidding but there was an edge in his voice. He meant to claim her and to do it as soon as possible.

Feeling a desperate need to change the subject, she motioned down to the laptop. "I've been working on this for the last few hours. It's tight programming. Your guy was no slouch. But I've gotten in a few layers."

"He was in the army with me. He did computer stuff. He decided to convert three years ago. He was an asset to the

Pack." And a personal friend. Pushing aside his pain and feelings of failure, he realized she wasn't wearing her glasses. "Don't you need your glasses?"

She blushed. "Oh, well. That was a disguise. Or not a disguise really, but a way of keeping from being noticed. I don't have to wear them, they're clear lenses." She pushed her hair back over her shoulder and he struggled to breathe.

Deciding to be nonchalant he moved in, needing to be nearer so he could get her scent. He wanted her to be as insane with longing as he was. "Oh, clever. I like you more this way, though." He knelt next to the chair and leaned in to see the screen and watched her fingers fly over the keys. "What is it? What have you found so far?"

Oh my god! He was so damned sexy and he smelled so good. She wanted to lean in and breathe deep of him. Pull his essence into her senses. Ugh! The man drove her insane. With a slightly shaky voice she answered, "It's encrypted. I've broken through three of what I can tell so far are six levels. The code it's in is pretty complicated, it looks like something I saw once at the Department of Justice. One I get past all of the built-in defenses and the traps, I'll unlock everything and then I'll have to see where to go from there."

He raised an eyebrow. "The Department of Justice? As an employee?"

She gave him a look and went back to the keyboard. "Something like that. Look, I'm not always proud of what I have done. I'm a different person now. I've worked really hard to be."

He snorted. His little human mate was full of surprises. "Are you hungry? Why don't you come down and grab something to eat?" *Or we can get into bed and I can fuck you boneless.* His eyes devoured every inch of her. His wolf pushed, strained within him to possess her.

"I will in a few minutes. I'd kill for a cup of coffee," she said, not taking her eyes from the screen. If she looked at him again she'd lose it.

"Okay, I'll get a pot of coffee on and start breakfast." He stood, and as he did he leaned in and inhaled her, his eyes sliding partway closed as her essence floated through his system. She turned and their eyes locked, her lips parting in surprise at the connection between them.

With a growl, he took the laptop from her, laying it on the carpet at her feet. He knelt between her thighs—those sweet, soft, bare thighs—and slowly brought his lips to hers. She stiffened for about three seconds and then relaxed into him. Her hands softly rested on his chest, his own hands momentarily still against the flesh of her inner thighs.

His tongue slipped into her mouth and she gave a soft moan, her fingers digging into the muscled skin on his chest. He nipped her bottom lip and she made a soft, startled sound—a mewl—sliding her hands up into his hair as he angled his head to taste her better.

She sucked at his tongue and it was his turn to moan as his cock throbbed in agony. She was warm and soft and perfect—made to be in his arms. Her taste exploded through him, her essence lighting every single nerve in his body on fire for her. And for her alone. He knew that now for an absolute certainty. Knew that she made him feel like no other woman had ever done before and this was just from a kiss. There was an overwhelming feeling of rightness in having her lips beneath his own.

He scented her wetness and slid his hands up her thighs. She parted her legs wider, giving him access to her sex. His thumbs slid over the now-wet panties and she arched into him, one leg rising to curl around his thigh.

Desire roared through Nina as she opened her legs to him. She felt as if she'd die if he stopped touching her. Her nipples were throbbing, pussy wet and hot and clenched, desperate to be filled. His lips tasted so good she felt drunk from them. They were firm and masterful and he knew just what to do. His large hands had slid up her thighs and she mewled in delight, barely stopping herself from moving down to meet them halfway. She'd thought that was good but when he moved his thumbs over her pussy through her panties she thought she'd lose it and come immediately. It had been so long, nearly five years, since she'd been with a man. *This* man was seriously dangerous to her peace of mind. She felt as if she were outside of her body watching someone else as she rolled her hips and begged for more with her whimpers.

He nibbled down her jaw as one hand came up to unbutton her pajama top, slipping inside to cup her breast. His palm slid over that hard point of sensitive flesh and drew back to pinch a nipple between his thumb and forefinger. He could smell her layered on his scent in the shirt and it drove him crazy. Her head lolled back and she gave a moan of pleasure that shot straight to his groin. His control was hanging by a thread at that moment.

"God, I want to fuck you," he growled and took a nipple in his mouth at the same time as he slid a finger into her panties and up into the heat of her clutching pussy. He felt the triumph rush through him as she gasped and moaned. Her honey scalded his hand. "Jesus, you're so tight, so tight and hot."

Clutching his head to her, her breath caught as he bit down on her nipple. Unable to resist, she moved her hips against his stroking fingers. Wanting more. She clutched his head to her as he gently bit down on her nipple and caused her breath to catch and then moan out loudly, moving her hips against his stroking fingers.

"Lex? You around?" Cade's bellow from downstairs shocked her back to her senses. Lex's growl around her nipple stopped her from her attempts to sit back up.

"Lex! You have a call from New York," Cade yelled out again.

"Go! He's going to come up here any minute." She squealed as he pinched her clit between slippery fingers.

"I can't leave you this way," he murmured.

"Lex! Damn it, it's important," Cade called out again, the frustration clear in his voice. She could hear him coming closer, footsteps getting louder. Feeling panicked, she grabbed his wrist and pulled his hand out of her panties and pushed him back, panting and irritated.

Sighing, he brought his fingers to his lips and licked them, eyes falling shut at the pleasure of her taste. "So sweet. This isn't over," he promised and adjusted his ridiculously hard cock in his pants and limped out of the room to deal with his call.

She sat for a few minutes trying to pull herself back together. What on earth was wrong with her? What was he doing to her? When he touched her it was as if everything else seemed to disappear. It was as if he was the only thing that mattered, and that was dangerous. She didn't have the time or the emotional energy to deal with a relationship right then. Ugh! And a man like Lex Warden wasn't really relationship material to begin with. She could just fuck him out of her system and then move on, but she had the sinking feeling that sleeping with Lex would not be something easily walked away from. She needed to get laid, plain and simple. She tried to tell herself that it could wait until after she had some distance between herself and Lex, but she knew it was a lie.

* * * * *

She ordered herself to suck it up and got dressed. She pulled on jeans and a T-shirt and made a mental note to stop at the mall and get some new clothes on her way back from the police station. Her hair was a lost cause. She put it into a loose braid that was already coming undone because her ponytail holder had snapped the night before.

Giving herself a stern talking-to, she took a deep breath, and clutching her case and the other laptop, she headed downstairs to the kitchen.

Trying not to show how much she enjoyed seeing Lex there cooking and holding out a mug of steaming coffee to her, she kept her focus on her laptop, setting it on the bar. She put the other case down and made sure the programs were still running before she looked up to him, grabbed the cup gratefully and sat down.

"Thanks," she murmured, putting her gaze back on the screen. If she ignored him, perhaps they could just forget that scene in the bedroom even happened.

He pushed the laptop aside and put a plate filled with bacon, hash browns, eggs and toast in front of her. "Eat."

She gave him an annoyed glare but dug in heartily, realizing it had been quite a while since she'd last eaten. Moments later she could feel the delicious food begin to energize her, and she needed that strength to meet the day.

Cade strolled in and grabbed a mug of coffee and sat at the bar with them. He did a double take, eyes widening as he took her in. "Uh, wow, who are you?" He laughed and it got even louder when he saw the look Lex threw at him.

Nina explained the situation quickly and Cade sent a surreptitious look at his brother and then back to her. "Well, I think glasses are sexy but I have to say that the you you've been hiding is pretty hot. I can see why you wanted to keep things low-key. I do look forward to hearing just exactly what it is you're hiding from someday."

"Put your eyes back in your head while you still have them," Lex growled.

Cade chuckled and looked back at Nina, who was blushing. He winked at her and tipped his head toward the laptop that was on the counter. "So? Any news?"

She took a sip of coffee and turned the screen to face Cade. "I've broken through some major security protocols but

I'm still working on the encryption program. Right now there's a program running through my laptop, hooked up to this one, that's trying to break through. The problem is that the protection program on this is layers deep and much newer than the program on my computer. Whatever your boy found out, it's something pretty major. This is really sophisticated stuff." She looked to them and narrowed her eyes. "You guys running guns or drugs? If you are, say so now because I have enough trouble and I don't have any need to borrow more."

"No! What is it you think a Pack does anyway?" Cade asked, offended.

She made an annoyed snort and waved in Lex's direction. "Look, your brother here carries a mighty big gun and seems pretty comfortable around ass kicking. You live in this very posh mansion, you drive a Mercedes and a Harley. Your clothes are designer. You're both wearing expensive watches." She stood up and began to pace, trying to stay calm.

"My brother was infected on purpose in a bar fight by one of your own Pack members. He pretty much has been off the radar for the last two years. I have no idea what you do but if he had a part in it, I can only guess that it's shady."

Lex gave an inarticulate growl of offense. "We don't run guns or drugs, Nina. The Pack owns a construction business. By trade I'm an architect but I handle Pack security. I carry a gun because sometimes we have to deal with dangerous situations. Cade runs the Pack as well as the day-to-day business stuff from the construction company and our coffeehouses. The Pack owns a coffeehouse in Queen Anne and another in Bellevue. Carter, the third-in-command, runs the coffeehouse in Queen Anne, and our fifth, Melissa runs the one in Bellevue. Nothing illegal."

She sighed. "Nothing you know about. This level of encryption doesn't protect coffee-buying records of your Pack, Lex. Whatever is on this hard drive is hot. Two people have been killed to protect it."

"As far as I can tell, you're the only one here who is a criminal," Lex said and immediately regretted it when he saw her wince.

"Yeah? Huh, cause no one's been murdered over me. I'm not carrying a big gun. My house—the house I had before *your* people torched it—wasn't protected by a sophisticated security system." Her voice was tight.

"In any case, if I recall correctly, we aren't talking about my past. This isn't about me. I've changed. Everything I did, I did to eat and to feed and house a teenaged brother. I don't have to defend myself to you," she bit off and he watched her close up. She moved her body away from his and it brought a frisson of panic from his wolf.

Lex winced, horrified that he'd hurt her. "You're right. I'm sorry. That was uncalled for. Some money has disappeared. Cade noticed it about six months ago. We also noticed that some non-Pack-affiliated wolves had been coming to our Howls. A few of the Pack hierarchy came to me, concerned that one of our own might be up to no good. We took a few names, discreetly, off the financial stuff, to try and protect the Pack. We didn't want to arouse suspicions or make false accusations but it wasn't something we could ignore. Tommie was watching three people for us."

"And they are?"

Lex looked to Cade, trying to decide how much to tell her.

"Hey look," she said, putting her hands on her hips. "My brother *died* for this crap. I'm either in or I'm out, there is no in between. You tell me everything or I'm out of here. You can crack your own computer—which you won't be able to."

"You aren't Pack, we don't share this kind of thing with outsiders," Cade tried to explain.

She widened her eyes at them incredulously. "Look at me, Cade Warden. Look at my face. Is this the face of a woman who cares? No! Listen, in fact, I could not possibly care less about not having the secret wolf handshake. I'm telling you how it's going to be. Take it or leave it."

Lex sighed, looking to Cade, who nodded his permission to tell her. "Sit down and finish your breakfast. Tommie was watching Carter, Melissa and Eric. They're all in the top Pack hierarchy, right below Cade and me."

"Obviously you don't know who Tommie was meeting that night."

He shook his head. "No, we do, but that's the problem. He met with all three of them that night. They all admit to having seen him but they all said that he left without a problem. According to their stories, Melissa was the last to see him, but obviously the killer is lying and so we don't know what the heck is up."

She nodded. "Okay, well, let me get back to work and see if I can't find some answers for you. I've got to go to the police station in an hour so let me get this program started so that it can work while I'm gone." She shoved her plate away, pulling the laptop back in front of her.

"While *we're* gone," Lex said.

"Do you always do that growl thing?" she asked, annoyed that it turned her on as much as it did.

"Are you always this difficult?" he countered, leaning in closer to her.

Before she could retort, Cade threw his head back and laughed so hard that he cried. Lex snorted, tossed the dishtowel at his brother's head and turned to gather up the dishes.

* * * * *

She tried not to cry when she saw the ruin of her house. Lex wanted her to see it before they went to the police. He hated hurting her but he wanted that emotion to help her because the last thing he needed was to bring more problems into her life than they already had. The cops and the arson investigators from the fire department needed to see how upset she was, needed to know that she didn't do this herself.

"I'm sorry," he said quietly as she looked at the ruin that had once been her home.

She shrugged. "There's nothing you can do. It is what it is." Her voice was flat but he could feel her sorrow. He wondered, not for the first time, just what it was that made her so distrustful. He also winced as he remembered his comment about her criminal past back at the house. He doubted she'd be opening up to him about that any time soon.

He touched the back of her hand briefly and drove her to the police station.

They were both relieved that their story about spending the night together was accepted without incident. They didn't have a lot to go on but the chemicals used as an accelerant were unusual enough that the attentions of the investigators had been raised.

"I know who you are, Mr. Warden. Do you think this might have something to do with your, uh, species affiliation? After all, Ms. Reyes is a florist, why would anyone torch her house?" The lead police detective on the case asked.

"I certainly hope not, Detective Stoner," Lex said calmly. Humans knew about werewolves, but there was an uneasy truce at best. "But you may be right. In any case, Nina is staying with me at my home, where I can be assured of her safety."

"That's probably a good idea." Stoner watched them both with the eyes of a very sharp cop.

Lex breathed an inward sigh of relief when the rest of the investigative team from the fire department came into the room and one of the men was clearly Pack. A look passed between the two and the subtle lowering of the man's eyes let Lex know that he accepted Lex's position.

They gave their statements and then to the insurance company agent who'd visited the site. Until the situation was investigated more thoroughly, Nina knew she wouldn't be seeing a dime from them. Thankfully she had a comfortable enough savings to deal with her living situation until that came through without having to touch her secret account. But it made her uncomfortable nonetheless. She'd lived hand to mouth and she had no desire to ever do so again.

* * * * *

On the way back to the house she made Lex stop at a local mall so that she could get some clothing and toiletries.

He did the typical man thing with that hangdog—she giggled to herself at the word—face as she shopped. Finally, two hours later, they emerged laden with bags of clothes, shoes and other necessities, which he loaded into the car without complaint. Vocal complaint anyway.

"I can't believe you took so long," he grumbled as he loaded the bags into the back of the car. There were few things worse than shopping, in his opinion. Even watching Nina Reyes pick out panties wasn't enough to make up for the misery of the mall.

"Well excuse me! My fucking house was torched because of some shady shit your people got up to! I had two pairs of pants, two shirts, a pair of sneakers and one extra pair of underwear. I don't have some big giant mansion with Mercedes in the garage."

She stood there, nose to nose with an alpha wolf, hands on her hips, eyes flashing.

Lex looked at her, watched her chest rise and fall with her breath, watched the fire in her eyes. God, she was magnificent, and every inch his equal. He pulled her to him and his lips crushed down on hers as he growled in frustration. At first she was stiff in his arms but within moments she softened and her hands slid up the wall of his chest and into his hair.

Her tongue shyly touched his lips and then possessiveness roared through him as her taste filled his senses. His mouth opened and he coaxed her tongue with his own. His hands kneaded her ass, the tips of his fingers moving toward the heat between her thighs.

She moaned at the pleasure of being in his embrace and had angled her head to kiss him more fully when a series of beeps sounded. Lex stiffened and then groaned as he pulled back from her.

"What?" she murmured, eyes slightly glazed.

He pulled a small phone out of his pocket and answered it, all the while moving her toward her side of the car. "I know," he grunted into the receiver and snapped it closed.

He opened the car door and motioned with his head for her to get inside.

"What? Why did you stop?" she asked, confused.

"We're standing in the open. It was stupid of me to let myself get carried away," he said as he gently but firmly pushed her inside the car and closed the door behind her.

He walked around to the driver's side and got in as she sat there, openmouthed at his comments.

Carried away? He groped *her!* He kissed *her!* He started it and he refers to that kiss as being carried away? Nina ground her teeth in frustration. She got the out in the open part—that was logical to be worried about—but *carried away?* Ugh!

Lex's nostrils flared. He could scent her anger and her frustration. "What are you mad about now?" he asked, agitation clear in his voice.

She turned on him, her arms crossed tight over her chest. Her eyebrows shot straight up with incredulity, her mouth opened but she closed it again. What on earth could she possibly say to this insufferable jerk? She snorted, turned back around and looked out the window without making a comment.

He tried to get her to speak a few more times but she just acted as if he didn't even exist—and oh how he hated the silent treatment. He only got it from human women. Well, female humans and his sisters. Other than that, female wolves accepted his dominant nature and didn't question it. Damn it! All of the beautiful and docile Pack females and his mate is a prickly human? Figured.

"Fine, be that way," he mumbled and pulled up the drive to the house.

She mimicked him with her head turned, not giving him the satisfaction of getting a rise out of her, and when the car stopped she got out and went to the trunk, waiting for him to unlock it.

He came around and opened it and moved her out of the way with his body. "Don't be silly. Let me carry the bags."

She tsked and moved back, motioning toward the car.

He carried the stuff up to her room and put it down. "Look, I've offended you somehow and I'm sorry. I thought you wanted me to kiss you. You certainly seemed disappointed when I stopped. After this morning, I thought that we…well that we had some major chemistry and I…"

"I'm not mad about the kiss!" she exploded. "It's being characterized as a mistake that I have a problem with."

"What? I never said it was a mistake to kiss you!" He began to stalk toward her and she moved back.

"You said it was stupid!" She squeaked as her back hit the door and she had nowhere left to go to escape him. She could feel the heat radiating from his body, could see the gold ring around the pupil of his eyes, could smell his skin.

"I said it was stupid to let myself get carried away," he said softly, leaning in and caging her with his body. "I've been doing this for a very long time, I made a rookie mistake by forgetting myself in a public place like that. I left us both open to attack. *That* was stupid. But I lose my head around you. When I touch you, smell you, I forget everything else."

His voice was so deep and low that the vibration of it slid down her spine and she had to close her eyes against it. "Oh." Jeez! Could she be any less articulate?

He chuckled and her nipples tightened. "Cade saw us come in. He's going to come up here and want a report on what happened." Regret in his face, he took a step back and cleared his throat. He also had to adjust himself—she took him from zero to rock-hard in two seconds.

Nodding, she smoothed down the front of her jeans. She walked around him to deal with the clothes she'd just purchased. He made her feel shell-shocked every time he touched her and then moved away. What was going on? It had to be grief related. That was it, grief related! It was about losing her brother and she was seeking out comfort from a man. That explained it. Satisfied, she nodded her head once and continued dealing with the packages and bags.

* * * * *

After Lex left to go deal with Cade and she put her clothes in the washer, Nina sat in the cheerful, bright eating nook in the kitchen for the rest of the afternoon, drinking coffee and working, her face a mask of intensity.

Her program had found some weaknesses in the security and she had been systematically taking it all apart for the last two hours. "Oh! You thought you were so clever, didn't you?" she mumbled.

Lex came up behind her and kissed the back of her neck. "What?"

"Stop that," she said, but he wouldn't move back. Sighing, she pointed to the screen. "A honey pot."

He slid a hand down her belly to press a long finger over the seam in her jeans, against her swollen clit. "This honey pot?" he asked in a whisper against her ear.

She grabbed his wrist and moved him away but that didn't stop him from noticing her hardening nipples. He grinned to himself.

"No! Get over yourself already. Ego much?" She pointed to the screen. "This honey pot. It's a program designed to look like something good, like what we're looking for. Only it's a trap. You open it and a virus eats everything on the hard drive or locks up critical programs."

"So what do we do then?"

"We don't open it. I'm almost done, or I think I am. Give me another hour," she said, dismissing him.

He moved away from her with regret. Sitting back at the table, he scanned the plans for a home he'd been commissioned to design. Since Cade was working from home to be nearby, Lex could be an architect for a few hours, put his gun aside. Before too long, he lost himself in his work and time ceased to exist for him.

* * * * *

"Lex," she called out two hours later.

He looked up and walked over to her, rubbed the back of her neck, pleased that she didn't try to shy away. "What is it, love?"

"Well, it's several things." She pointed to the screen. "These numbers…"

"Shit, those are Swiss bank account numbers," he said, leaning in, interrupting her.

Cade came into the room. "What's up?"

Besides the very hard cock poking at his zipper? Lex motioned to the screen. "She's in. It's Swiss accounts."

Cade came to look over her other shoulder.

"Okay," she began as she flipped between screens of data, fingers flying over the keys. "These are Swiss accounts and those are dates of transactions and the totals moved. Don't know what currency, that's not noted, but let's assume dollars."

"Holy crap! If it is dollars, there's quite a lot of money there," Cade said with a whistle.

She pointed at the screen. "Yeah and money going out too. Lots of it. Someone has an expensive lifestyle."

Cade looked at Lex and frowned.

"Jeez, you've got millions here coming and going. Within days of a transfer in, there's transfers out," she said as she worked.

She clicked to another screen.

"What on earth is that?" Cade asked, looking at the string of numbers and letters.

"Something they didn't want anyone to see. I think this is what the security was for," she murmured as she entered a long string of code and hit enter. The numbers and letters coalesced into something else. "It looks like a formula of some kind."

"Jesus, that's the lycanthropy virus," Lex breathed out.

"The what?" Nina asked, alarmed.

"Why would Tommie have this?" Cade asked as Lex continued to rub the back of Nina's neck.

"I don't know but it can't be good. He said he had something big but he couldn't say more, there were people around. All I know is that he was supposed to meet with me later that night after he'd met with the others." Lex looked to Nina. "We've known that lycanthropy is carried as a virus that can infect humans through contact with blood. Recently our scientists isolated it and began to try and work on ways to protect the immune systems of humans. So if they were infected against their will, they could take some kind of anti-viral blocker right after exposure. It's still experimental but shows a lot of promise."

Nina made a face. "Yeah, well. Too late for Gabriel. Of course, if you isolate the virus you can also use it to infect people. Hell, you can make it in large doses and contaminate something shot directly into the system—something as innocuous as a flu shot. Or you can use the anti-viral agent to attack werewolves, causing their system to attack itself," Nina said.

"The Rogues," Cade said simply.

"But why?" Lex ran a hand through his hair, clearly frustrated. "We need to find out just exactly is going on. Rogue wolves usually just get involved with petty stuff, nothing too bad. Certainly not at this level!" He paced as he thought. "You can't just accuse a Pack member of something like this without proof, without any real idea of just exactly they are up to and why."

"Use me as bait," Nina said.

"No." He rounded on her, fixing her with a glare.

"Why? Lex, it could work. You make it known that Gabriel's sister is around. That there's a laptop with information on it. We see if we can draw them out, if they try and grab me. They might tell me what they're up to if they think they're going to kill me."

Lex looked utterly incredulous and threw his hands in the air. "Oh my god! Could that be any more of a sitcom plot? Why wouldn't they just shoot you in the head like they did your brother?" Lex demanded and then felt immediately sorry as she winced. "I'm sorry, I didn't mean it to come out like that."

She waved it away. "You're right. I just thought of a better idea anyway. Still bring me around the Pack but leave me alone with the three prime suspects. We can let it be known that I was with Gabriel when he was killed, see if anyone approaches me for information."

"This is over your head. You're a florist, for god's sake!" Lex exclaimed.

"First of all, I was running scams when you were at keggers at Kappa Kappa Werewolf. You don't know much about me but I am way smarter than Gabriel was. I'm a consummate liar. I can street fight with the best of them and I can cheat at cards like nobody's business. This on top of my computer skills. I may not howl at the moon and have superhuman strength but I can hold my own."

"Whoever this person is, they are ruthless and dangerous. I don't want you in danger," Lex said, trying not to order and not to plead, knowing neither would work with her.

"This person murdered my brother. That makes *me* ruthless and dangerous. Plus, they're up to something that is akin to bioterrorism either against humans or your own kind. Something has to be done and this is a good plan, the best you've got." She said this emphatically. She wanted him to see how necessary her presence was to the situation.

"She's right, Lex," Cade said. "We have to expose her to the suspected parties just to see what they'll do. You'll have backup on her the whole time."

"I will not ask you to risk your life," *not when I've finally found you.* His wolf pressed against his conscience, demanding that he protect her.

"You're not asking. I'm offering. Lex, Gabriel may not have been an exemplary citizen or anything, but he was all I had. He was my brother and I loved him. This guy can't be allowed to get away with it." Nina looked into his eyes, pleading.

He let out an explosive breath. "Nina, I don't want to get you hurt. Can you understand that?" He couldn't help but implore her to be safe.

"Lex, I know and I appreciate that. But you have no other choice." Nina said this with finality and he accepted it. It was that or have her go off and try this stupid plan of hers on her own. He may have only known her for a brief time, but he didn't doubt that she would take matters into her own hands if she felt she had no other choice.

He threw his hands in the air in defeat. "Fine. But we do it tomorrow. After some planning. Nina, you are too tired to carry it off right now."

"All right. We'll do it tomorrow." She didn't want to push her luck. She'd obey him. For the time being.

The moment stretched out between them and she started to speak when Cade interrupted. "I think I'm going to fire up the barbecue for dinner."

"I think I'll take a nap," she said. She closed the laptop and headed up the stairs to the guestroom.

"That's fine, hon. It'll be about two hours before we eat. I'll come get you when it's ready," Cade called out and she thanked him over her shoulder.

Leaning against the closed door she sighed deeply, trying to calm herself. What the hell was going on with her anyway? It wasn't that she didn't like sex, it was just that sex came attached to men and men were trouble. She had her battery operated boyfriend and a handheld showerhead, and those had been fine until Lex Warden had lumbered his way into her life.

"Argh!" she hissed and her head banged against the door. "Stop this!" she ordered herself and pushed into the room. Telling herself to get a grip, she pulled off her jeans and slid into bed.

Of course, all she could do was think about the kiss in the parking lot. The way he'd felt with his hands and mouth on her earlier that morning. The way he made her lose her head in the tide of hormones he seemed to evoke.

She lay there and tried to sleep for the better part of half an hour, tossing and turning and trying not to think about the fact that she was wet and horny and that she ached to have him inside of her. Finally, with a sigh of frustration, she sat up, threw the blankets back and rolled out of bed.

But before she could even reach her jeans there was a tap on the door and she knew who it was.

* * * * *

Lex watched her take the stairs with a sexy sway of her hips. She probably wasn't even aware of how sensuous she was with those big brown eyes, those lush lips and that long hair that hung ever-so tantalizing just above her heart-shaped ass.

Cade turned to him once her door closed. "What are you waiting for?"

"She needs to rest," he said gruffly. "She's had a hard few days."

Cade rolled his eyes and pushed his brother toward the stairs. "Your wolf wants to claim her. She's getting ready to do something dangerous and if you don't mark her, you won't be able to concentrate with her around all of those other wolves."

"I'm not a wolf right now," he tossed back as he began to walk up the stairs.

"You're *always* a wolf, Lex. What's more, you're an alpha wolf, a warrior," Cade said quietly and went back to working on the meat, effectively dismissing him.

Lex paced around his room for half an hour. He wanted to let Nina sleep. She was tired and upset over Gabriel's death. At the same time, he wanted her more than he could wrap his head around. Cade was right, he could feel the wolf just beneath the surface, pushing him to mark her, to claim her as his woman. Once he came inside of her she'd be marked as his. His biological stamp would be on her and a bond would be forged. She wouldn't be happy with anyone else and neither would he. They'd become integral to each other.

Making his mind up, he left his room and walked down the hallway. He stood at the head of the stairs and looked down, seeing Cade in the kitchen whistling and cutting up vegetables, the tray of uncooked meat marinating on the counter.

He went to the door to the guestroom and tapped quietly. If she were sleeping she wouldn't hear him anyway.

She opened the door and they stood, silently staring at each other for a few moments.

"Nina..."

She grabbed his hand and pulled him inside the room, shutting and locking the door behind herself, leaning on it for strength as she took him in.

He pulled off his shirt and she greedily drank in the details of his upper body. Strong, thickly muscled, not an ounce wasted. Not too much muscle—what was there wasn't for show. It was the body of a man who worked out. Not just a body but a tool. Danger poured off him in waves—he was a big, bad man and she wanted an extra helping of it. She wanted to eat him up in great gobbling bites until she was positively stuffed with him. Oh he made her weak in the knees!

She took one step, then another until she was standing very close, then reached out a hand to stroke over his chest. She leaned in and closed her eyes as she took a deep breath and had to reach out to hold on as she nearly fell over with the intensity of her reaction.

Her body tightened up, nipples stabbing the front of her shirt, skin flushed and heated. Her pussy bloomed with desire, her honey making her slick. The world became a pinpoint of focus. Suddenly it was just the two of them, nothing else existed that mattered but having him inside of her body.

Lex gripped her forearm to keep her standing. "I know. It'll pass in a moment."

She looked up at him with widened eyes. "You know? What do you mean, you know?"

"I feel it too. The first time is the hardest, but each time I get a deep whiff of you, it nearly knocks me to the ground. I get so frenzied with lust that I have to grind my teeth to not drag you to the nearest horizontal surface and plunge inside of you."

"What is it?"

He pulled her shirt off and unhooked her bra and they both hissed out when bare skin met bare skin. The feel of those diamond hard nipples—so pretty and delicious—pressing into his body made him delirious with want.

"Pheromones."

"What?" This was slurred as she became drunk with him. Her eyes slowly slid closed as his hands moved up to cup her breasts, pinching her nipples between clever fingers.

"Chemicals, personal chemicals. Yours call to me, mine call to you." He leaned down and kissed the spot just below her ear and she moaned.

"I know what pheromones are! But that's mumbo jumbo. You're just horny, I'm just horny. It's not science." Even as she said it she didn't believe it. The totality of what she felt for him—the way her body responded when he touched her—it was more than mere horniness.

He made a *tsk* sound with his lips against her skin. "Liar. You know what I'm talking about and you know it's the truth."

"So if we fuck this…intensity will lessen?" She was breathless as she asked.

"It will always be intense, Nina. You're my woman. Once we're bound the intensity of our connection will deepen." He said this in between pressing kisses down the long line of her neck.

She ignored that and arched into the questing hand that reached into her panties. She turned off her brain and just felt. Opened herself up to sensation. It was time that rational, by-the-book Nina went away for a while so Nina who hadn't been fucked in years could get some.

Her hands slid down his chest and found the waist of his jeans and she yanked them open, satisfied as she heard each pop of the long row of buttons releasing. Suddenly he was there in her hands. Hard, velvety smooth and so hot. She encircled him with her fingers and looked down, smoothing a thumb over the head where a bead of semen pearled. He moaned and watched as she brought her thumb to her mouth.

He was salty, musky, masculine.

She squeaked in surprise as he picked her up and stalked to the bed, tossing her onto the mattress as he shucked his jeans and climbed up, halting on all fours above her, looking down into her face.

"Do you give yourself willingly to me?" he said, his voice low and laced with desire.

She writhed beneath him. The heat from his body blanketed her. She could smell him, the clean salt of his skin, the woodsy scent of his cologne, beneath it, the elemental Lex that she'd come to...oh god. She shoved that thought away quickly with rational Nina.

She nodded. "Yes. Oh god, Lex, please. I need you inside of me right now." She didn't even recognize her own voice, it was sultry, smoky.

"All in due time. I need to taste you. All of you." He started by taking her lips again in a kiss that was designed to melt her, to make her bones jelly, and it was a good thing she was lying down because she didn't think her legs would have supported her — he was quite successful.

He kissed down the line of her neck and she ran her fingers though his hair like she'd wanted to since she saw him that first night. It was so soft and she could smell his shampoo.

He stopped at her breasts, rolling his eyes up at her and she watched, entranced, as his teeth scraped over her nipple and his tongue swirled around. Over and over until she was nearly panting. Each draw of his mouth shot straight to her clit until her pussy was clenching and unclenching in time with his mouth on her nipple. Oh how she wanted him inside of her!

Stopping and pulling his mouth back, he gave her a grin so sexy and devastatingly naughty that she gasped. She watched down the line of her body as he kissed over her stomach and breathed hotly against her neatly trimmed mound. His big hands slid up from her calves to her inner thighs. His broad shoulders held her thighs apart. With another one of those grins, he moved down a bit and settled between them.

It had been so very long for her. Four years since her last date and five since she'd had sex. And even then it was a brief affair—he had been horrible in bed. She began to feel self-conscious. She knew for sure that the man between her thighs was experienced in bed. She had only slept with three men in her life and none of them provided her with any noteworthy moments. She was extremely limited in her sexual experience.

Embarrassed, she tried to close her legs against him, but he pressed his palms against her inner thighs and pushed, holding her open fully to his gaze. "No, beautiful. I want to see you. All of you."

"I, uh, well, ohmigod…" She broke off incoherently as he put his mouth against her pussy, taking a long lick from anus to clit.

"You taste so good, Nina. I don't know that I'll ever be able to get enough," he murmured, looking up at her with those deep green eyes.

"Uh," she managed. Her head fell back against the bed and he chuckled and went back to work.

He lapped at her with long, slick strokes of his tongue, tasting the landscape of her pussy, learning her body as she herself learned. Not that she'd ever admit it to him but she'd never been given oral sex before and man oh man had she been missing out!

Over and over he licked. He nibbled and laved and lapped at her. While his fingers slowly pressed into her pussy, he flicked the tip of his tongue over her clit. He ate at her like she was the best thing he'd ever tasted and it made her feel like a goddess. She'd never felt anything quite so intense in her whole life.

It was so incredibly intimate, his mouth there on her. The way he was so big and feral and yet utterly gentle with her moved her deeply, despite the fact that she did not want to be moved.

She focused instead on the sensation of his mouth—his tongue, wet and soft as it stroked over her, his lips moving against her labia, over the hood of her clit—it made her delirious with pleasure. Her orgasm began to settle into her body. She could taste the metallic presence of it on the back of her tongue. She could feel it filling the empty spaces in her body, expanding, building until it burst over her in what felt like a shower of sparks. Back arched, hands fisted in the sheets, his name burst from her lips as she exploded into a climax so powerful it felt like it was filling up and then wringing out each and every cell in her body.

Before she could drag her eyes open she felt him move up her body and begin to press his cock into her still spasming pussy.

Lex was drunk with the taste of her body. With the way she responded to him. She was so wet and she tasted like something he'd never even imagined. So good and so right that he couldn't quite wrap his head around it. Each moan and gasp and sigh she gave him shot straight from his cock to his heart. Her desire for him was a powerful thing, it wove a spell over Lex and he felt bound to her already.

He moved up and positioned the head of his cock at her gate. Her eyes slowly came open and she smiled up into his face. It was an utterly unguarded moment and he had the feeling that was a rare thing with her.

"Hi. Don't you need a condom before you do that?" She said in a purr as an elegant brow slid up.

Oh hell no! In the first place, werewolves didn't carry human STDs. In the second place, he could scent that she wasn't in the fertile part of her cycle. But lastly and most importantly, he needed to come inside of her to mark her, to claim her. He wanted that, no, he *needed* that.

"We don't carry STDs and you aren't at your proper time for pregnancy," he said as he began to push deeper. She was creamy and soft and swollen but really, really tight.

"Ah," she said with a wince. He was pretty impressive size-wise and it had been a very long time since that territory had seen a penis.

"Damn it, Nina," he said through clenched teeth, "you're so tight. It's so good I might come before I get halfway inside." A horrified look broke over his face. "You aren't a virgin are you?"

She laughed. "No. But it's been a while. Why, you have a policy against virgins?" And she broke into a moan of pleasure as he began to stretch her more fully.

"No. I just don't want to hurt you."

"I'll let you know if that gets to be a problem. Now shut up and fuck me."

He looked down into her face with surprise and then threw back his head and laughed. This woman was pretty damned amazing.

Inexorably, he pushed into her, the superheated, tight walls of her pussy clutching at him, parting for him like a molten curtain of flesh. His teeth were clenched as he concentrated on keeping it slow. He wanted to slam into her to his balls, wanted to feel her embrace fully and right then, but he could feel the truth of her statement that it had been a while. He'd never been with a woman so tight before and he was afraid he would hurt her.

Pulling her legs up high, she brought them under his arms, opening herself to him more fully. Rolling her hips, she pulled him in further. "More. I'm going to die if you don't get deeper."

He watched as a bead of sweat from his neck fell onto her chest, and that suspended moment burned itself into his memory. He locked eyes with her and slid completely in to the root, gently bumping her cervix, and they both responded with a sigh of pleasure.

"God, you feel so good, Nina. Your body was made for me," he whispered in her ear.

She laughed and realized that she hadn't felt this good, this relaxed, in a very, very long time. Safe. "It certainly feels that way, doesn't it?"

"I think we need more testing," he growled and began to drag himself out of her and thrust deeply again. Over and over, her body received his. Her hands were at his shoulders, fingers digging into the muscles there. He could feel the blunt edge of her neatly trimmed nails against his flesh. He could smell the lilac of her soap and shampoo, the clean scent of her sweat, the tang of her sex.

Her body was made for his. Cunt to cock, they were something more than two people and something less. They were, for want of a fancy phrase, one and more than the sum of their parts. The silken walls of her pussy gripped him, embraced him, the soft skin of her inner thighs slid against his ribs as the sweat of their endeavor slicked the way. Her hair was spread about her face and head on the pillow and he noticed the flecks of amber in her eyes.

He leaned down and dipped the tip of his tongue in the small dimple to the left of her mouth and he felt it get deeper as she smiled in response.

"Come into me, Lex. Come inside of me," she said softly, almost shyly. It was the last straw after the tightness of her pussy, the sinuous drag of her sweat-slicked body beneath his own, the soft moans and sighs of pleasure she made each time he pressed back into her body. He was going to complete the claiming, make her his own by marking her.

The primal nature of this pulled his wolf closer to the surface and he arched back and gave a silent roar of her name as he came hard and deep within her. Within his woman. Over and over, his cock pulsed as he poured his life into her.

Long moments later he collapsed to the side, careful not to fall on her. He reached out and pulled her to his body and she sighed happily and snuggled into his side.

Seconds later though, she opened her eyes, pushed back and sat up, looking down into his face. "What the hell did you just do?"

Chapter Three

ഇ

She said this as she fell back to the mattress and gut-wrenching shudders broke over her. Her teeth began to chatter.

He sat up, concerned, and leaned over her. "Nina? Baby, are you all right?"

"Does it look like I'm all right to you?" she demanded through teeth clenched to keep them from chattering. "What is going on?"

"I uh, I think it's the claiming," he said as he got up and went into the adjoining bathroom, coming back quickly with a wet washcloth that he put on her face, mopping up the sweat that had gathered there. "It shouldn't be like this. Only, well, I've only known wolves who did it to other wolves. But I know there are humans who mate with wolves and they seem fine…"

Before he could continue to babble she whacked him upside the head with the pillow to shut him up. "What the fuck are you talking about? Claiming? Mates?"

"I've told you before, you're *my* mate! I'm *your* mate! I just completed the claiming. It's my seed inside of you that does it. If you were just some random woman, it wouldn't be a big deal but because you're my mate, the woman who is my biological match, my DNA is now twining with yours in a sense."

Despite his fear for her, he smiled softly and his voice gentled. "I can feel it too. Only it doesn't hurt, really. I just feel incredibly connected to you. And wow, you're not happy with me at all are you?"

"You're *altering* my DNA?" Despite her shivering, which was lessening, she sat up. "Oh my god! Without asking me? You've done something to alter my fucking humanity without asking me?"

He put out a hand and touched that luxuriant brown hair and despite herself she leaned into his hand. She didn't just want that touch, she realized with a start—she *needed* it.

"No way! Nina, I *told* you up front about the bond, about you being my woman. I asked if you gave yourself willingly to me and you said yes."

"You didn't say you were changing my DNA! I thought you were trying to get into my pants."

He raised an eyebrow at her. "If all I wanted was a quick fuck, I'd have had it weeks ago. This is more than that and you know it. This is forever. You and me, Nina. We belong together. I didn't trick you into this. I told you up front and you agreed. Furthermore, you *know* I'm telling you the truth." He was not going to allow her to get him mad. No, he felt great, damn it, she was his woman and she was bound to him and he to her.

Grrr! She hated it when he was right. He had asked her, but how could she have known his semen was some kind of wonder-jelly-magic-DNA-changing stuff? She was silent as she thought it through. She examined her feelings, and beneath her anger she realized she felt connected to him in a really deep way. She felt a part of something, of someone, in a way she'd never allowed herself to imagine. Did she want to have some mystical hoodoo with this man? Ack! With this werewolf? "Well, it's too late now. What's happening? What does this mean?"

"Nina, baby, look at me," he said and gently tipped her chin so that she was looking up into his face where she couldn't ignore the truth of the situation.

He saw the panic in her eyes and his heart ached. "Do you really think I'd do anything to hurt you?"

She shook her head, afraid if she tried to speak she'd cry. Now that the shaking was over she was drowning in emotion. She'd never felt anything like what she was feeling at that moment. It was as if the warmth of him was seeping into every pore. She felt his presence, his confidence and courage, his strength, his desire, his lust and his fear. His love. God, he loved her. How in the hell could he love her? Worse, she felt the same. Oh god, she was doomed, she was in love with the giant tool. She actually *liked* this feeling of connection. Gah!

"What is this?" she managed to croak out. "What's happening?"

"I feel it too. It's the bond forming. We don't have detailed explanations for it. All we know is that when a male releases his seed into his mate, the bond forms. An emotional and physical connection is made."

He leaned down and kissed her gently and his own fear ebbed when she responded.

"Great. Magical cum, lucky me." She sighed and quirked up a smile at him. "So am I a werewolf now?"

He chuckled. "No. You'd have to have the virus put into your bloodstream through a bite. We can talk about that later but we have a lot to deal with right now just figuring out who killed Tommie and Rey. I want to focus on keeping you alive through this ridiculous plan of yours. Then we can talk about whether or not you want to be a wolf."

"We should start planning. How are you going to arrange this meet-up?" She sat up and he pushed her back to the mattress.

"We are not talking about any of this until tomorrow. Tonight you are going to rest. We'll get dinner and I'll get you moved into our room while you take a long hot bath. Cade will call the family together to accept you into the Pack as my mate, and my mother will be thrilled of course. She's always on me to give her grandchildren. Heh, Cade is next! The pressure is off me now..."

She put her hands over his mouth. "God, you seemed so stoic before you got your super semen into me. Let's back up, shall we? First of all, moving in together?"

"Nina, where else would you be?"

"Shouldn't we date for a while or something?"

He sighed and rolled on top of her. His weight anchored her as she smoothed her hands up the muscles of his back.

"Beautiful, you are my mate. Where else would you be but with me? Human mates live together, why wouldn't we?"

"Well, people date and then they sometimes live together and then they get married. They don't set up house after having sex once."

"I think we are having some basic problems with definition here. You are my mate. I am your mate. In human terms then—you are my wife. In werewolf culture, once a mate is claimed that's a declaration, a marriage. You carry my scent, Nina. A wolf will be able to tell that you're my mate by scent. I carry yours as well. There's no courtship, although you've certainly been a pain in my ass over the last weeks as I watched you, that's probably close to a courtship for a prickly woman like you." He said this last with that naughty grin.

"Married?" she asked faintly as she thought it over, giving his ear a halfhearted twist for the prickly comment. "Well, I'll agree to the moving in to the same room part, after all we're sleeping together and I don't have a house anymore, so my being in here is silly. But it's going to take me some time to deal with the marriage idea. Plus, uh, this mate thingy is fine for you in your culture and all, but humans don't recognize it, do they?"

He frowned. She was so contrary. "I don't care what others recognize. It is. You are mine, period."

"Yeah, okay, He-Man. So now you want me to meet your mother? 'Cause you see, I'm not exceptionally good with mothers. They never seem to be very excited when they meet me."

"Well of course! Nina, do you need to go to the doctor? Are you having hearing problems? You. Are. My. Mate. My mother and father and sisters are all going to want to meet you. And they'll love you. In fact, they have to meet you before anyone else in the Pack does or my mother will never let me hear the end of it." He rolled off her and reached for the phone and she grabbed his arm with a squeak.

"You're calling them now?"

He laughed. "No, Cade, as the Alpha, will call them. I have to call one of the Pack who is a jeweler, have him design rings for us."

She groaned, fell back to the mattress and pulled the sheet up over her face. "You know, Rushy McRushter, you don't have to go all wild right now. We can, oh I don't know, take things slowly!"

He leaned over and pulled the sheet back and peeked into her face. "Rushy McRushter?"

She gave a wave. "It was off the cuff, I'm better if I have time and I'm not being pushed into marriage by a fuck-drunk werewolf."

He laughed. "Fuck-drunk? Good one. But there's no point in not moving forward. It's a done deal." He shrugged. He dialed the numbers and she groaned and rolled out of bed in search of her panties. With a growl he pulled her back to the bed with an arm around her waist. "I have plans for you, don't rush off."

He held her there while he spoke to the jeweler and had him start on some design ideas for rings but swore the man to absolute secrecy under pain of death. He sounded so serious about the last part that Nina shivered. He was so big and bad and scary but she didn't feel threatened in any way by him. That was really sexy.

When he hung up he turned back to her and his lips moved toward hers. She gave a soft sigh until she heard Cade bellow up the stairs that dinner was ready.

Lex cursed under his breath and sighed.

"Let's ignore him," Nina murmured and pulled him back toward her.

He extricated himself from her. "As much as I'd like that, he'll never quit. He's an alpha, used to being obeyed. It's damned annoying sometimes but that's the way things go. He's mellow, but when he's spent hours cooking he'll be pouty if we don't go down there and ooh and aah over everything."

"God, you two are girls," she mumbled and got up. Failing to find her panties she put her jeans back on without them.

"You're awfully mouthy for such a beautiful woman," he said, catching her at the door and pulling her into an embrace.

"Yeah? Too late to complain, you bought the cow, even though I'd have let you milk me at least five more times."

He laughed and swatted her bottom as they walked out into the hallway. "You're going to keep my life interesting, I think."

* * * * *

Cade was putting the opened bottle of wine on the table when they walked into the room. He spun, nostrils flaring, and rushed over and pulled them both into an embrace. "Congratulations!" He kissed Nina's cheek. Lex growled at him and Cade gave him a raised brow and a smirk as he whisked Nina to the table.

"I'd better call them before we get started. If mom finds out we had dinner before I told her you'd claimed your mate she'll never let any of us hear the end of it," Cade said and grabbed the phone.

Nina snorted and grabbed a piece of garlic bread. Lex poured her a glass of wine and then one for himself and Cade.

The conversation was short and he returned to the table.

"Well?" Lex asked, a fork at the ready to spear a steak.

"They're on their way over. Let's go ahead and eat, it'll take them a while to get here."

"You know, maybe I'll just shower and change," Nina said, getting up.

"No. Nina, you need to eat. You've had a really rough few days," Lex said, putting his hand on her arm to stay her.

"Lex, I am not meeting your family in jeans and no makeup. God. I'll be back down in a few minutes." She narrowed her eyes at his hand and he removed it with a sigh. She caught Cade's pout and snorted. "Look, blossom, I'll be back in a few minutes, don't cry."

Lex gave a surprised bark of laughter and Cade sputtered as she jogged out of the room and headed upstairs.

Rifling through the clothes she'd bought earlier, she decided on a pale peach-colored pair of clam diggers and the cream tank that went with them. She took a quick shower, put her hair back in a long braid and dashed on some makeup. She examined the results in the mirror and shrugged, that was as good as she could get on short notice. She shook her head. She was meeting her boyfriend's, no, *husband's* family in a bit and she had no idea what they'd think of her. In the past, parents had never been overly thrilled with her. The class thing had been an issue and the race thing too. Sometimes blonde mothers were not happy to see their sons bring home a Latina. And when Gabriel got into trouble all the time, that was another factor.

She hadn't met anyone's parents in at least seven years though, so maybe it would be different. She was a business owner and used to be a homeowner. Respectable. She snorted at herself in the mirror and headed downstairs.

"Finally," Cade mumbled and went into the kitchen, bringing back a tray of food he'd been keeping warm for her in the oven.

"You look beautiful, Nina. But it's not necessary to dress up. My family is going to love you." Lex kissed her hand.

She snorted and began to eat, despite her nervous stomach. She hadn't eaten since breakfast and was starving. The last thing she wanted to do was faint when she met his parents.

"This is delicious, Cade," she said, meaning every word.

He smiled proudly. "Thanks. The marinade is something I've developed over the last ten years. I'm going to sell it to some of the smaller gourmet food shops in Seattle and Bellevue later this year."

She finished the delicious steak and veggies and limited herself to one glass of wine. Lex cleared the plates and refused to let her help so she sat with Cade in the large living room and looked out the wall of windows toward the city.

"Wow, you can see Bellevue and Seattle too."

"Welcome to our family, Nina. Truly," Cade said as he took her hand and sat next to her on the couch. "Lex deserves someone like you. You're strong, you'll stand up to him and anchor him too."

She smiled at him and squeezed his hand. "Thank you, Cade. I don't quite know what to say other than that. I don't even know what to think about all of this."

He laughed. "Yeah, I can imagine it's a bit overwhelming just now. And there's some more stuff that we need to talk about..."

"Not now, Cade," Lex said shortly as he came into the room and sat down on Nina's other side.

Cade sighed and got up to look out the windows. "It's too late anyway. Their cars are coming up the road."

"Too late for what?"

"We'll talk about it all later," Lex said, cutting off any further discussion.

"Cars? Plural? How many of them are there?" Nina's heart began to pound.

Lex put an arm around her shoulder. "My parents, my grandmother, two of my sisters, one brother-in-law and their two children. Megan and Tegan are here already, they're in Cade's guard."

"What? Jeez, that's a baseball team! And Megan and Tegan?"

"They're twins. They'll come up when everyone else does. You'll like them."

"Wow, your mom is a fertile Myrtle!" Nina placed her palms flat over her stomach, almost protectively.

Cade and Lex laughed and she went to the windows and watched three cars pull into the large drive and park. The cars spit out ten people, all beautiful or handsome and very well dressed. The children looked to be about seven and nine and they waved toward the windows and headed into the large yard while the adults headed inside.

A tall, lithe, silver-haired woman walked in first, followed by a burly man with dark brown hair and big green eyes, and at his side a petite redhead. Another couple followed and then two younger women who appeared to be around Nina's age.

"Grandmother," Cade said with a grin. He embraced the silver-haired woman and turned toward Nina and Lex. "This is Nina Reyes."

The woman narrowed her eyes and looked Nina up and down to the point that she wanted to run, but instead she squared her shoulders and stood tall. She had nothing to be ashamed of.

The woman saw it and a smile broke out over her face. "Fortune has blessed you, Alexander my boy." She walked to Nina and took her hands. "Welcome to the Pack, Nina. Welcome to our family, I'm pleased to meet you."

Relief rushed through Nina and she smiled back. "Thank you, I'm pleased to meet you as well."

Lex turned her to face his parents. Cade motioned to her and spoke to his mother and father. "This is Nina, as you can scent, he's formed the bond and claimed her. Do you accept her into the Pack?"

The man stood forward and cocked his head. "Lex, you smell content."

Lex nodded. "I am."

The woman moved beside him. "She's strong? Can she be the mate to the Enforcer of this Pack?"

Cade spoke this time instead of Lex and Nina was beginning to get exasperated, feeling like they'd start looking at her teeth any minute. "I watched her deliver a roundhouse kick to a full-grown werewolf two nights ago. Surrounded, facing the death of her brother, she continued to fight, never showing any sign of giving up. She stood up to Lex as he kept her under surveillance for weeks. She even managed to elude him while he was tailing her."

The man raised an eyebrow at that and Lex made a growling sound but didn't contradict the story.

"Will she accept her wolf?" Lex's mother asked Lex.

"She and I will discuss that later. Right now there are bigger issues," Lex said solemnly. He could feel Nina beginning to get impatient with everyone talking around her.

"And she knows and accepts all aspects of our culture, then? The tri-bond included?" His father asked.

"We were just about to discuss that when you pulled up," Lex said this quickly and Nina turned and narrowed an eye at him.

His father sighed. "Lex…"

"I said we'll talk about it later." Lex's tone brooked no further discussion. "She is my mate, you can clearly see that. She's beautiful and intelligent and strong. She's mine and that's all there is to it."

His mother smiled at that. "Nina, I'm Beth Warden, this is my husband Henri. Welcome to our family. The next weeks will be very confusing as you become immersed in our world.

Please don't hesitate to come to me or to my mother or your sisters-in-law for help. You're one of ours now." She kissed Nina's cheeks and stood back.

His father stood forward and kissed her forehead. "Welcome to Cascadia Pack. You are one of our own now, Daughter." He turned to Lex and pulled him into an embrace. "You've been blessed, Lex. She's going to be good for you."

There was a general lessening of tension then and Nina was presented to Lex and Cade's sisters and brother-in-law, who all seemed quite happy to meet her and eager to welcome her into the Pack.

While Cade was telling his father about the situation with the laptop and their tentative plans to draw out the killer, Nina leaned over and hissed into Lex's ear, "Don't think I've forgotten that you aren't telling me the whole story."

He winced and then kissed her temple. "I'd never dream of it."

The family stayed until well after midnight, talking and laughing. Lex refused any talk of how to go about catching the killer, admonishing them all over Nina's wellbeing. Instead they spoke about Pack business.

Henri had been Pack Alpha and before him it was his father. He'd stepped down ten years before, and handed the reins to Cade.

Lex had been in the Army and served as Ranger for eight years after that, which had trained him even further. He'd gotten his training as an architect while in the Army. He returned to Cascadia when he felt truly ready to take his place as Enforcer, when he was twenty-eight. The same year Cade became Alpha.

She wanted to hear more about his reputation as the "Big Bad" but Lex got embarrassed and made them stop so Nina whispered to his sisters that she'd talk to them at a later time about it.

Chapter Four

After everyone had been seen out, Lex turned to Nina. "Why don't you go and get ready for bed. Relax a little, read one of those books in that stack you bought today. Now that everyone is gone, I can finally move your things into our room."

She smiled. "Twist my arm."

As she got to the top of the stairs she looked back down at the two brothers. "Don't think I don't know you two are going to talk about whatever the hell you've been shushing everyone up about all night, Lex."

Cade chuckled and Lex rolled his eyes.

After she'd gone into their room and the water turned on as she brushed her teeth, Lex motioned with his head and Cade followed into the guestroom, where they began to gather up her meager belongings and moved them quickly into their suite.

She was still splashing around in the bathroom when Lex sat down in the living room. He looked over at Cade with a sigh.

"You have to tell her, Lex. Explain it."

"She's human. I'm concerned about how she'll take it."

"Yeah, and you don't want to share her." Cade's perceptive eyes studied his brother.

"I'm not sharing her! It's one time and only because it's necessary. Don't get any ideas, Cade." Lex pushed off the couch and began to pace.

Cade stayed seated. "Do you think I'd try to take your mate from you, Lex? Do you think so little of me after all?"

Lex shoved a hand through his hair. "No. But she's gorgeous. Perfect. How could you not want more?"

"Lex, she's yours. That right there is enough for me. But the tri-bond must happen. You know it and I know it. And it has to happen soon, as the bond forms. She won't be able to handle it all if we don't do it." Cade wanted Nina, she was attractive and strong, but she belonged to Lex and that was that.

"Not tonight. It's late and she's tired and she's had a big day. Let me have her to myself for just a bit longer." Lex leaned his forehead against the window.

"Tomorrow morning, then. You know it has to happen. Now go to her. Call me when you're ready in the morning."

Lex nodded shortly and went upstairs after her.

He let himself into the bedroom and stood for a moment, breathing in the smells that she brought with her. Her scent was married with his. Her clothes hung in their large closet. Her presence was there, part of his. He smiled as he saw her propped up in their bed, reading a book.

"Hi there," she said with an almost shy smile.

"Hi yourself, beautiful." He walked to her, put the book aside and pulled the clip from her hair. It tumbled about her shoulders in a sweet smelling rush. Taking a curl between thumb and forefinger, he rubbed it, delighting in how soft it was.

Her big brown eyes looked up into his and he pulled the covers back and smiled at the sight of her naked body.

"You're so damned beautiful. You know that?" he murmured and kissed her shoulder.

"Mmm. Thank you." Coming up to her knees, she reached out to pull off his shirt and yank the button of his jeans open. He moved her hands out of the way and did the rest himself, taking everything off as he stalked back toward the bed.

She fell onto her back on the mattress with a laugh and he followed her down.

He went in to kiss her and she rolled him over so that she was on top.

"That'll do nicely. Slide on up here and let me taste you." She blushed hot and he looked at her carefully. "You taste good, Nina. Heavenly."

"It's not that, although, thanks. I've never done it that way," she admitted quietly.

"You've never sat on a man's face?"

"Eeeek! And you say I have a bad mouth?"

"What? There's nothing dirty about you sitting on my face. Although you won't actually sit, more like kneel and I'll do the rest." He laughed and then he rolled back over with her on the bottom again. "If you feel uncomfortable we can try it another way."

"Why don't you let me taste you?" She hadn't done that very often but she liked it and it was something she wanted to do to him.

"We can do both. Turn around."

She must have looked confused because it dawned on him suddenly.

"Come here." He grabbed her and rolled again, his back on the bed. He turned her body so that she was astride him, her pussy just above his face. He could smell how turned on she was, how ready.

Before he could say anything, she took the initiative and pulled him into her mouth. He groaned at the pleasure of it. The heat, the wetness, the slick, sinuous slide of her tongue over his cock pulled him into a web of sensation the likes of which he'd never felt before.

She did not hesitate, instead sucked and licked him with gusto. He allowed himself a few moments to enjoy it before he opened up his eyes and held her open with his thumbs.

There she was, glistening and cocoa pink, swollen with her desire for him. Her clit was there, peeping out of its hood and he slid the tip of his tongue over it. She jumped in surprise and then moaned and rolled her hips back when he did it again.

Her ass was perfect. Round and fleshy but tight, he could tell she walked a lot. He wanted to bite into it and he would at another time. The pretty pucker of her rear passage was there and he couldn't resist a swipe with the flat of his tongue. She gave a surprised gasp and tried to move forward but he held her there, strong hands at her thighs.

"I want all of you, Nina. Every last inch of your body," he growled possessively. She mewled in pleasure when he followed that statement up by pressing his thumb into her pussy and swirling his tongue over her little hole again, then nibbling on her perineum and around his thumb, tasting her honey.

She tilted her hips, giving him better access to her pussy as she continued her erotic assault on his cock. He then ate at her, laving and licking, nibbling and sucking until she was trembling and her rhythm on his cock was off. Her body was slowly moving back and forth on him as she sucked his cock and before long she was grinding her pussy flesh into his face without hesitation.

She was moaning low around his cock, the vibrations traveling up the shaft and through his balls, up his spine. He didn't want to come in her mouth, he wanted to be inside of her again and so he knew he had to push her into orgasm first.

Fingers digging into the flesh of her ass and thighs, he quickened his pace, fucking into her with his thumb. He latched onto her clit and sucked slowly in and out over and over until her head shot back with a gasp and she cried out his name as her orgasm, quicksilver, rushed through her body.

Nina was still surfing the relentless waves of her climax when she felt Lex move out from under her. He murmured for her to stay there on her hands and knees and another intense orgasm pushed through her cells as he nudged his cock into her cunt.

"Oh god, that's so good," he gritted out as the walls of her pussy rippled around him in climax. She was creamy and soft and it felt so damned good to be buried inside of her that way he was sure he never wanted to leave.

Her honey coated his cock and he watched himself pull out and then press back into her. In this position, his wolf was very close to the surface. Strands of her hair lay across her back in big fat spiral curls. It partially obscured her face but he could see that she'd caught her bottom lip in her teeth.

"I've wanted this since that first night, when you pointed that damned shotgun at me. When you looked like some spinster. When I smelled your room I was a goner," he whispered.

She thrust back at him. "You looked at me for half a second and decided I wasn't fuckworthy, don't lie," she gasped and then moaned.

"You grew on me. But honestly, I began to fall in love with you when you flipped me off," he said with a laugh and she laughed too.

Had he ever laughed in bed with a woman before? Had he watched his cock disappear, gripped by the lips of her pussy? He couldn't remember, and there'd been a lot of women before her. It was as if her presence in his life, in his bed, had erased all other women from his head.

He slid his palms up the curve of her waist and leaned forward, cupping her luscious breasts, the nipples stabbing at him. "You're everything, Nina. Everyfuckingthing to me."

He saw her lips curve in a smile and she made a contented squeal as she slid back and met his thrust. Over and over, the wet sounds of their union echoed through the room and the scent of their sex hung in the air. It wove a sensual spell through his senses, the bond deepening with each plunge his cock took into her.

He felt his orgasm begin to tingle, arc up his spine, skitter over his scalp. His fingers tightened and she grunted a bit, not in pain. It shot out of the head of his cock in wave after wave and he let a growl go and pulled her closer and bit down on her neck, holding her in place while he fucked into her with feral intensity. His wolf roared close, he could feel it just beneath his skin, and when she met that feral intensity with a growl of her own he let go of her neck, reared back and gave a triumphant howl.

They both collapsed to the mattress, and he felt her slip consciousness and fall into sleep, his cock still pulsing inside of her.

* * * * *

Nina awoke to the sounds of murmured conversation. She turned over and saw the place where Lex had been sleeping. She rolled over and soaked in his warmth, his scent. The man was a heater. She'd woken up cold and had just snuggled in close, his arms had come around her and his heat had blanketed her immediately.

She smiled. She shouldn't be feeling this way, but she did, and for once in her life she was just going to go with it. What she had with Lex Warden was amazing and deep and the best thing she'd ever felt.

Lex came back into the room and she gave him a lazy smile. He was wearing low-slung pajama bottoms and she watched the ripple of his muscles as he came to her. Her smile faltered when she got to his face. He looked tense, worried.

She sat up. "What?"

He heaved a sigh. "You remember last night you said you wanted to hear the whole story?"

She nodded.

"Can Cade come in? He and I both need to explain it all."

She leaned over and grabbed his T-shirt from the night before and pulled it on, keeping her naked butt under the covers. "Okay," she said warily.

Lex moved to her and kissed her forehead and lips. "It's okay. This won't change anything between us. Believe that."

"You're scaring me, Lex."

"I'm sorry, beautiful. I don't mean to. I love you."

"Just get him in here and let's get this over with."

He nodded and moved to the door. Cade came in and sat at the foot of the bed. "Morning, Nina."

"Morning, Cade. Now, tell me what's going on. I'm sure my imagination is only making it worse than it really is."

Cade laughed but it was strained.

"The bond between mates is really strong. Wolves, in their natural state, mate for life. Did you know that?"

"I think I read something about that a few years ago."

"Well, with werewolves it's the same. We mate for life. The claiming and the establishment of bonds between mates is at the cellular level. And the higher status a wolf has in a Pack, the stronger the bond is."

Nina nodded, not seeing where the hell this was going.

"So you know that Lex is Second in this Pack, right below me?"

Nina raised her eyebrows, showing impatience. "Yes. Where is this going?"

"Okay so the deal is that when werewolves mate, they have something called the tri-bond. It's to establish an anchoring bond for two really important reasons. First, so that the female won't lose herself in the emotional and hormonal surge of the claiming, and also to keep her alive should something happen to her mate."

"Tri-bond?"

"Well, you bonded with Lex. Now you need to bond with another wolf. That bond will stabilize your connection to him, keep you safe."

She pulled the sheet up higher. "Bond? Like how?"

"Like you bonded with him."

Narrowing her eyes, she jumped out of bed and began to pace, forgetting that her butt was naked beneath the T-shirt she was wearing. "Like I bonded with him? You mean fucked? I'm supposed to fuck some other wolf to *save* myself? Oh and does he get to fuck someone else to save him?"

"Nina..." Lex began, standing up.

"No! Answer the question!" She stopped in front of him, her hands on her hips.

"No, I'm not going to have sex with anyone else. It's just for the female of the bonded couple. We don't know why it works that way but it does."

"Let me get this straight. You want me to fuck another man?" Cold hurt replaced the warmth of connection she'd felt when he'd first come into the room.

"No! Damn it, I don't. I don't want anyone else touching you, but we have no choice. Nina, without the anchor of the tri-bond you'll drown in the sensation of our connection. It will slowly overwhelm you until you can't handle it anymore. Those females who didn't have to be institutionalized have killed themselves over it. And even if you could overcome that, I have a dangerous position in the Pack. If I died you'd follow me. The tri-bond will save your life! Do you think I want you insane or dead? I love you, Nina. I want to protect you." His voice caught and she shook her head.

"And you didn't see fit to tell me about this before you *claimed* me? Oh yes, you didn't ask to claim me either! And you love me but you want to share me?" She spun and yanked open drawers until she found her clothes and began to put them on.

Lex stood there. He could feel the pain knifing through her and as such, it knifed through him too. He didn't want her to be with anyone else but it had to happen to protect her. She was right to be angry that he hadn't told her.

When he saw her reach for her bag and begin to toss clothes into it, he sprang into action. "What are you doing?" he asked, grabbing the bag.

She reached for it but he tossed it to Cade, who opened the door, threw it in the hall and closed the door, his back against it.

"What the hell are you doing? You can't keep me here!"

"You can't leave, Nina. In the first place, it isn't safe for you out there. In the second place, the tri-bond needs to be sealed today. It's dangerous to let it go much longer. The longer we're bonded the worse it will be." Lex tried to pull her into his arms but she pushed him off.

"Oh so my substitute fuck is here? Where?" She was sarcastic until she saw Cade against the door and it finally dawned on her.

"You have to be kidding me! You two lure me up here to wolf mansion and now, *oh gee,* I have to fuck you both or I'll go crazy? Has this worked on other women? Oh my god, what a fool I've been. I actually fell for all of this mate stuff."

Lex growled and grabbed her upper arms, hauling her to him gently but firmly. "You are my mate, Nina. You can't deny it. And there is no other woman. You're it! You know this is real. Stop lying to yourself, stop lying to me." He was desperate to make her see the truth of it all.

"Lex, why don't you give us a few minutes." It wasn't a request. This was the Alpha speaking. Lex growled at his brother but felt compelled by his Alpha.

"I'll be just outside the door, baby. We will work this out," he said and went to the door. "Don't hurt her, Cade."

Cade growled low and menacingly and Nina pressed herself back against the dresser in reaction. "How dare you,

Alexander? Do you think I would hurt any member of my Pack without reason? Do you think I would harm your mate? Get out into the hallway, now."

Lex gave her a look back over his shoulder and left the room.

"Sit down, Nina."

"He may cow to you but I don't. I'm not a werewolf, you're not my king."

"Have it your way." He sat down on the bed. "You're hurting him, you know that don't you?"

"What?" she asked, incredulous. "I'm hurting him? The man who fucks me and then comes into the bedroom and announces that I'm supposed to have sex with his brother? I hurt him? Puhleeze!"

"Oh cut the tough act. I can see how upset you are. But to answer your question, rhetorical though it may be, yes, you hurt Lex. He doesn't want this, Nina. He loves you. But it's the only way."

"Oh, and what a sacrifice for you," she said sarcastically.

He sighed. "Let's cut the shit shall we? Total honesty. On one level, I hate this because he's my brother. He's taken a bullet for me. He spends his life protecting me and this Pack. That he's found you is a wonderful thing. It grounds him in a world that's chaotic with violence and threat. So yes, on that level it is a sacrifice because I have to do this and it hurts him.

"On another level, I am very attracted to you. Part of it is that you're an alpha, even if you are a human female. In many ways a warrior. Because you are mated to my brother, chemically, my attraction to you is very close to a mate connection. It won't be hard for me to bed you on that level. I'm hard right now just thinking of it."

Nina stared at him, mouth agape.

"It has to happen. I'm not lying. Lex isn't lying. Hell, you can call my grandmother and ask her about it. All females who are mated to wolves need the tri-bond. And as a human it's even more urgent. Lex tells me that you had a very severe reaction after the claiming—that concerns me. And as your Alpha—and I am your Alpha, Nina—and Lex's brother, I'm driven to do what's best."

"Get out," she said through clenched teeth.

"Nina, be reasonable."

"GET OUT!" she screamed and threw a vase at his head, which just barely missed him.

Lex opened the door and saw her, standing legs apart, fire in her eyes, rage running through her system. "What the hell is going on?" he demanded.

"You and your brother need to get out! Get away from me right now. I can't stand to look at either one of you."

"Okay," Cade said, his hands up, palms out. "Think about this, Nina. Think about your feelings for Lex. Do you think he'd lie to you? Be honest with yourself. It doesn't have to be some long seduction, you know. He can be in the room with us. We'll figure it out. Do it in the way you feel most comfortable with. I know this is hard to take in. Just examine your heart."

He stepped back and pushed Lex out of the room behind him. She slammed the door in their faces, locking it.

* * * * *

Furious, Nina paced as she thought about the whole series of events. Damn werewolves were nothing but problems from the moment they materialized in her life. They turned her brother then they killed him and now she was trapped with these men who just so happened to *have* to both fuck her to save her life.

Gah! Men! She never should have let him into her bed. She had been weak and look where it got her. She stomped into the bathroom, slamming and then locking the door. She may as well shower the scent of that asshole off her skin while she thought of a way to get out of there.

96

* * * * *

"I'd ask you what you said to her but I heard you through the door. This is more than just duty for you, Cade," Lex growled as he paced.

"Control your wolf or I will," Cade said with menace. Lex had partially transformed twice in the last half hour. Cade had never seen his brother lose control this way. "Yes, it's more than duty. I will enjoy fucking her. Is that what you wanted to hear? I wish it weren't true but it is. Nina is a very alluring woman. But I know who she belongs to, Lex. I would never step over that line and you know it."

"God, can't you two do even this right?"

They both spun and caught the entrance of their youngest sister, Tracy.

"Thank god you're here!" Lex said.

"Where is she?"

"Upstairs in our room. She's really angry and hurt."

Tracy examined both of her brothers. So strong and handsome, if they couldn't convince a woman that it would be a great idea to have sex with both of them she didn't see much hope for the next generation of the Pack. Dumb as stumps. She snorted.

"Well, you claim her without telling her the details and then you spring, *hey, you have to sleep with my brother to keep from going crazy,* on her after a night of what I'm guessing was lovely post-bond sex. Really. First Sid handles Layla all wrong and they nearly break up and then you go botch this."

Lex glowered at her. She was the little rebel of the Pack. Tattoos and piercings god knew where. "Are you going to help or not?"

She rolled her eyes. "Of course I am. But you don't think I'd miss the chance to give you both some shit over it do you?" She turned and left the room without waiting for an answer.

Shaking her head in disgust, she jogged up the stairs and stopped outside Lex's door, tapping softly. "Nina? It's Tracy. We met yesterday? I'm Lex's youngest sister. Can I come in, please?"

"Why? Do I have to have sex with you too?" came from the other side of the door.

Tracy laughed at that. She really liked her new sister-in-law. She had all the fire it would take to keep Lex in line. "No. Are you disappointed?"

The door yanked open and Nina was there, looking imperious right down to the single raised eyebrow. "What do you want?"

"Oh come on and let me in. You know you're curious. What do you have to lose?"

She sighed, waved Tracy into the room and relocked it after her.

Tracy opened up the bag she had with her and tossed Nina something. "Here, it's a sandwich. Chicken salad. Thought you might be hungry after Frick and Frack sprang the tri-bond on you without warning."

Nina sat on the bed and gestured for Tracy to do the same. "Thanks."

"No problem. There's chips and a cookie in the bag too," she added as she opened up her own sandwich and began to eat.

"Why are you here? I don't mean to be rude, but let's just be blunt."

"You know why I'm here." She looked up at Nina. "Lex called me in a panic and I rushed over. Come on. Admit it. You know, deep down, that Lex and Cade aren't lying. I bet you're feeling a bit shaky about now. My sister Layla didn't want to do the tri-bond either." Tracy tucked her feet beneath her as she ate. "Anyway, so she and Sid had sex and the claiming happened. Only they didn't know they were mates, they thought it was just a lust thing.

"Lay flipped out! She didn't want to be mated to anyone, much less an artist. Sid's a painter, by the way, he's quite good. Anyway, so she tried to walk out on it. Even growing up in a Pack and knowing about the necessity of the tri-bond. He tracked her down with his cousin and she raged all over him about it.

"But it didn't change the facts and after three days she had to admit it. She was starting to slip control of her emotions and she was generally losing it. Sid was just about to involve my parents," Tracy rolled her eyes, "when Lay finally allowed the tri-bond to go forward."

Tracy leaned forward and took Nina's hand. "I know you love Lex. What will happen with Cade can be fun, or not, but it has to happen. I won't say it'll be meaningless because you'll be connected to him in a deep way, but it won't be the same as what you and Lex have and it will save your life. It'll save Lex's life too."

"What do you mean it'll save Lex's life?"

"He didn't tell you, did he?" Tracy snorted. "When you lose it mentally, you'll drag him down with you."

"He didn't say," Nina said faintly.

"And what does that tell you?"

"He didn't want to use that to force me into a choice."

"That would be my guess. He's pretty sensitive for such a tough guy."

"He's a tool."

Tracy looked surprised for a moment and then laughed so hard tears ran from her eyes. "Yeah. But he's your tool. What are you going to do?"

Nina sighed. "Why didn't Layla come?"

"She's carpool mom today. And we thought that I'd be the best person to talk to you about it. Plus, I like you."

"I like you, too. Did that hurt?" Nina asked, pointing to the ring in Tracy's eyebrow.

"Nah, not as much as the nipple ring."

Nina laughed. "Let me finish this sandwich and then I'll get around to having sex with Cade. I can't believe I'm actually complaining about that. If it weren't for Lex I'd be all over him. And oh, I suppose that's pretty icky for you to hear."

Tracy smiled. "Yeah, well, no need to go on about it. They're both handsome wolves. 'Nuff said."

Half an hour later Tracy came down, tossed the trash in the can under the sink, looked at her brothers and sighed. "Go on, I fixed it for you. And a tip for the future? Just tell her up front or she's never going to be able to trust you."

With that she gave a wave and headed out the door.

"Well, let me go up first. Then follow in a few minutes," Lex said to Cade as he started out of the room toward the stairs.

Cade nodded and went back into the kitchen.

* * * * *

Lex tapped on the door and called her name softly. She opened it and motioned him inside.

Nina saw the pain on his face.

"I'm sorry, baby. I really am. I didn't want to spring this on you, hell, I didn't want it to be at all but it can't be avoided and I know it's unfair and you must hate me but I love you and it's necessary and we'll get through it…"

"Babbling again," she said and put her finger over his lips. "It's just once, right?"

He nodded.

"Okay. Can we just get it over with then?"

He nodded again and moved her finger away. "Do you want me in the room?"

"If you're not in the room will you imagine all sorts of things?"

He thought about it for a moment and nodded.

"Are you sure you can handle being in the room? Because I want to remind you that I didn't bring this up. This isn't sex with someone else for recreation. I don't want to be punished for it later."

He took a deep breath. "I'd rather be in the room than not. And I know. But I don't want this to be like a medical exam for you either. I've been thinking and I want you to enjoy it. As it'll be the only time you'll be with anyone but me, let's just make the most of it. You'll be bonded with Cade, not in the same way as we're bonded but still, I think it's best if an emotional bond can form, too. Since we'll all live in the same house, even after he mates, we should make the best of this thing."

She raised a brow dubiously but nodded. They both jumped when there was a tap on the door.

Cade came in and the tension rose in the room. "Ready?" Lex and Nina nodded and Cade held out his hand. "What shall we do?"

Lex explained quickly that he'd be staying in the room. He and Nina hade decided to let the experience play itself out naturally instead of being something clinical.

After a bit of negotiation that had Nina giggling in parts, the two brothers turned to her. She sucked in a breath at the sexual intent in their gaze.

Suddenly her giggles were gone and she wanted to fall back on the bed and spread her arms wide while she called out, "Take me now!" No way could she be nonchalant about this.

Lex stalked over to her and pulled her body against his own. She could feel the heat of his skin, the pounding of his heart under the palm she had flat against his chest. She looked up into his eyes and felt their connection soul deep. He was her heart, the coursing of blood through her veins, the muscles, the bones. He was part of her in a way that was beyond her ability to even articulate to herself.

He bent down and captured her lips with his own, pulling her into a kiss that devastated her. His lips were firm and strong, warm and full of life. He poured everything he felt about her into that kiss and she took it. Soaked it in, received every bit of emotion, let it fill her up. In turn she fed it back with her own kiss, her hands nearly reverent on his chest.

Cade watched them both, feeling the intensity of what they had together, feeling love for his brother and this mate of his and no small amount of envy. He wanted this for himself, wanted a mate bond that would hold him, fill him. Complete him. He was forty years old and it was high time.

Lex broke the kiss and met Cade's eyes over Nina's shoulder. He turned her slowly to face Cade.

Nina nearly gasped as she caught the look of raw hunger on Cade's face. He looked like Lex but the lips were a bit more full, his eyes were hazel instead of green and his hair was more blond than brown. An aura of power emanated from him, she could feel it rising like heat from the pavement.

Lex pulled the shirt she was wearing over her head and then slid her bra off. Her nipples pebbled against Cade's greedy gaze and in response to Lex's large hands cupping her breasts, the thumbs brushing over the dark pink tips.

Her head fell back against the wall of Lex's chest and Cade moved forward. He fell to his knees, his hands at her waist, opening her jeans and sliding them down with her tiny panties. She reached out to hold his shoulder for balance when she stepped out of her clothes, and the spark of connection traveled up her arm.

Turning his head, he brushed his lips across the pulse point of her wrist and she gasped softly.

Lex moved so that his lips were at her ear. "Come back to the bed, beautiful."

She allowed herself to be pulled back and laid on the bed. She looked up at them both and watched as they pulled their clothes off. Cade was taller than Lex but his muscle wasn't as dense. He had a thicker pelt of hair on his chest and down the line of his abdomen than Lex did and his legs were longer. And his cock, well, she had to try and not stare but it was thick, meaty and had a swing to the left. And it was happy to see her.

Ah, the bounty that greeted her eyes! She'd gone from no sex in years to this? Damn! Yes indeed, the bitter with the sweet. The ache of her recent loss played up against the exhilaration of this joining of lives she had with Lex.

Lex looked down at her, at her smile, the way her hair spread out about her head, her high, full breasts, the curve of her thighs and stomach. Her deep olive complexion. She was so beautiful, so sexy and desirable. At that moment he felt proud of her, this exceptional woman who was his, as he shared her with his Alpha, his brother.

Cade crawled on the bed, between her legs, and kissed his way from the back of her knee up the ultra-sensitive skin of her inner thighs, coming to a stop at her pussy.

Lex leaned down and kissed her lips and down her neck. She arched and gasped as Cade used his thumbs to part her labia and took a lick and then another.

"So sweet," he murmured against her flesh. Lex chuckled around her nipple and then bit down just on the edge of gentle.

Where Lex ate her pussy with long slow licks, Cade flicked her clit relentlessly with the tip of his tongue while he fucked her with his fingers. The first time he hit her G-spot she nearly came off the bed.

"Ah, I see I found something. Let's try that again," he said briefly and began to stroke her sweet spot every few times he thrust into her with a "come here" motion of his fingers.

Her legs began to tremble and she whipped her head back and forth. She was moaning and gasping and her hands gripped Lex's head to her as he moved from one nipple to the other.

"Let it go, beautiful. Show him how gorgeous you are when you come," Lex said softly to her, urging her on.

One of Cade's fingers, wet with her honey, slipped down and tickled around her rear passage at the same time as he scraped over her clit with his teeth. She arched with a cry as climax rushed into her, drowning her in pleasure. The shock of it lit her nerves and tingled through her body.

Lex held her tight and kissed her, pulling her gasping cries into his mouth.

Cade looked up and watched her come, watched the flush of desire bloom over her body. He saw Lex's face as he took her in, soaked in her pleasure and the beauty of the moment. He envied it.

"You ready for me?" he asked softly and she looked down at him, her eyes coming back into focus.

She looked back up at Lex, wanting to be sure that they were on the same page. "Are you okay with this?" she whispered.

"It's okay, baby. Just enjoy it." He kissed her forehead and looked at his brother, who had waited and then moved up her body when he saw it was all right.

Nina locked eyes with him and he moved her thighs up over his forearms and pressed his cock against her slick pussy, feeling the wet heat envelop him in a tight grip.

"Jesus, you're so tight," he said through clenched teeth. It was so good that the pleasure gripped his guts and spine. She was so luscious, so beautiful, that he was in sensory overload. He wanted to make it last but he knew that it wasn't his place. He knew that this was for the tri-bond and that this woman was not his, nor would she ever be.

He closed his eyes against her appeal and stroked into her. Her body received his with a rhythm older than time. Lex was behind her, his body curled around hers. Nina tipped her head back to see his face and then looked to Cade again.

It was beautiful and yet surreal. Lex was giving his most prized possession to his brother, even if on a temporary basis. He watched another man fuck his woman, he should have felt jealous, but he didn't. It was something as old as their culture and it was going to anchor her to this life, keep her safe and sane and with him. He knew that should anything ever happen to him that Cade's bond would see her through. That made him feel relieved and intensely emotional about it. His wolf was protecting his mate, it was primal and feral and *right*.

He knew, even as he watched Cade love his woman, she was his and that would not change. That enabled him to get past any jealousy and to embrace her pleasure and his brother's sacrifice. He could see the envy in Cade's face and he wanted very much for his brother to have this with a woman of his own.

"Oh god, yes. Harder," Nina said hoarsely and Lex's cock hardened at the sound. Cade groaned and began to thrust deeper and harder.

The slap, slap, slap of his strokes rang through the room, buffeted by her moans and sighs and Cade's heavy breathing.

Cade's cock felt so good. The cant to the left stroked over the walls of her cunt, firing those nerves that didn't get sparked with Lex. It was a different pleasure. The thickness of him made up for him not being as long as Lex was. It was intense and more so because he was doing it for a higher purpose. This wasn't just a fuck — not that it wasn't an excellent one — it was a brother doing something for a brother, an Alpha protecting one of his own. That touched Nina deeply.

He was kneeling, the wiry hair of his forearms tickled the backs of her calves, the tender flesh at the back of her knees. She reached up and touched his face. This couldn't just be some clinical thing for her. He'd given her so much pleasure with his mouth. He was going to bind her to him in a way and she wanted an emotional connection, even if it was just collegial.

He turned his face into her hand and kissed her palm and she could feel another orgasm hovering at the base of her spine, building there.

"Touch yourself, Nina. Make yourself come. I want to feel you come around my cock," he growled. She slid her fingers into his mouth for a moment to wet them and he watched as she moved her hand to her pussy, jumped as she gasped when her fingers found her clit.

She licked her suddenly dry lips and then began to slowly stroke herself. With her other hand she grabbed Lex's cock and he pumped into her fist. The three of them moved together, seeking pleasure.

Cade nearly blacked out when he felt the first ripples of her pussy around him. She was like a scalding fist gripping his cock. Her breasts moved enticingly as he thrust into her. Her dark nipples were puckered and he leaned down and licked over one and then the other and delighted in her mewl of pleasure.

He pulled back and watched her hand on herself, catching glimpses of the glistening pink of her cunt. He could tell she was close. Her breathing became short, he saw the muscles in her forearm cord as she increased the pressure and speed of her fingers on her clit.

With a long gasp she began to come. The muscles deep inside of her clutched at him, rippled and milked him, and it was more than he could take. Head back, he groaned as he unloaded his seed inside of her.

Lex followed them both and Nina felt the satin heat of his cum land on her side and hand.

She also felt the same thing she'd felt when Lex came in her the first time. Utter contentment and restfulness. And then the trembling and sweating began. Her gut clenched, waves of nausea hit her as her muscles twitched.

She vaguely felt Cade withdraw, but the cool cloth that wiped her face and forehead, and Lex cleaning her hand and side, brought her back. She opened her eyes and stared into Cade's and felt it. Yes, love for him. Not the same depth or intensity that she had for Lex, but love nonetheless. At the same time she felt, for want of a better word, anchored. As if the bond did indeed stabilize the out-of-balance feelings she'd had since bonding with Lex the day before.

"Are you all right, Nina?" Lex asked gently, pushing a curl out of her face.

She sat up slowly and leaned against the headboard. "Yes." She didn't want to say much more because she had no way to express the depth of what she felt for Cade without hurting Lex, even if she'd had the words, which she didn't.

"We should get planning, you know," Cade said, grabbing his pants.

"Yes." Nina felt oh-so articulate. "Cade?"

He looked at her and she knew he felt it too, and there was no need for words. He pulled his shirt back on.

"Thank you." It was simple but genuinely felt.

He nodded at her and then looked to Lex to be sure everything was all right between them, and was satisfied that it was. "Not like it was a chore." He laughed, breaking the tension.

She got up and went into the bathroom to shower again and Lex followed her after he'd hugged his brother and thanked him.

They didn't make love but he lavished her with attentive care, gently washing her as he laid kisses over her clean skin. In turn, she did the same for him. They needed the gentle moments to reestablish their connection after the tri-bond.

They came downstairs half an hour later, dressed and ready to face whatever lay ahead.

Chapter Five
ഹ

"Okay, I think we should go to the Pack house tonight. It's been a few days since we've been there and now that you're bonded it's your responsibility as a ranking member of the Pack to bring Nina around for everyone to see." Cade bustled through the kitchen as he talked.

Nina moved past him and grabbed some juice out of the fridge. She tossed one to Lex and handed another to Cade before hopping up onto a barstool to listen. A rhythm had been established and no one questioned it, it simply was.

"So, what then?" Nina asked.

"Well, I think all we have to do is say who you are, you know, what a coincidence, Rey's sister is Lex's mate! And then we can talk about how you met, how despite losing Rey we have this laptop and we're trying to figure out how to get in," Cade said.

"In fact, I think we should keep the computer whiz part to ourselves. Unless you have a record. If I were the killer, I'd have run a background check on you." Lex watched her as he fished for information about her past.

"My record was all juvenile stuff. I got smart enough not to get caught after I'd turned eighteen. My juvenile stuff was petty, no computer related anything. I don't even have internet access at home. There's no reason to believe I could crack it," she hedged.

"Have you been clean since you turned eighteen, then?" Lex asked.

She yawned. "I hope you're better at this when you're on the job. If not, you wolves must be pretty stupid."

"I have a right to know, Nina!"

"You don't have a right to everything of me when it concerns my past, Lex. It's my business. I told you I've been clean for seven years and that's the truth. That's all you need to know."

"What are you hiding, Nina?"

"Nothing, Lex! Nothing that means anything to anyone but me. Now drop it, studly, or we'll have to have our first fight. In the last hour."

Cade laughed and then quickly coughed to cover it as Lex threw a glare his way.

"Fine," he said through clenched teeth and she rolled her eyes.

"So back to planning. We'll go to the Pack house — what's that anyway, like a frat house for werewolves? A flophouse? Where you keep your chippies?"

"Chippies?" Lex grumbled. "I had no need to keep a chippy! And I'd hardly call a Victorian mansion with twelve rooms a flophouse. It's a communal house where we often meet. Many of our single wolves live there. We have offices there so that we can work. It's a way of establishing a familial atmosphere."

"Without getting werewolf hair on the two-thousand-dollar couch here?" she said dryly.

"Precisely. My father nearly died because he had no filters between running the Pack and his home life. He had a heart attack ten years ago, it's why Cade took over the Pack. He and my mother were barely speaking, which as you might imagine, is a serious thing for a bonded couple. Anyway, we have big gates out front for a reason." Lex wanted her to know he was planning to put their relationship high on his list of priorities.

"Okay so we go to the Pack house tonight and what? Hang out? Have some beers and I get to get dirty looks from all of your old girlfriends? Will the suspects even be there?"

He wasn't going near that girlfriend comment with a ten-foot pole. He knew enough about women to know that was a trap and he wouldn't go willingly.

"Yes, Melissa lives there and Carter and Eric will be there because Wednesday nights are gathering nights. There's a big dinner there, a sort of social. All of the single females will be around and Eric is always on the prowl," Cade said with a wry grin. Eric would be eminently pleased that Lex wasn't competition anymore.

"And these are your three suspects? You know it has to be one of them?"

"Well, the money that has gone missing came from accounts that only the Inner Circle of the Pack had access to. In other words, Cade, me, Melissa, Carter and Eric. No one else had that level of control or the ability to get into accounts. Tommie seemed very sure it was one of those three."

"Okay then. Let's go and see what we see, shall we?" She stood up and tossed the glass container into the recycling. "Nice. Eco-friendly wolves."

"You think she'll be accepted by the Pack?" Lex murmured to his brother when she got on the phone with the manager of her shop.

"I'd like to see the first wolf who tries to give her any shit," Cade said with a laugh. "Rey was easygoing and took a lot. I don't think this apple is from that tree."

Lex laughed at that. Yes, he thought she'd handle herself just fine, but if any wolf in Cascadia Pack even thought they could treat her as anything less than his mate he'd grind them into a greasy spot.

She came back into the room and looked them both over. Hands on her hips, she cocked her head. "A few things—first, I hope you had fun talking about me, punks. Second, I need to go to my shop starting tomorrow. Third, I want to plan a memorial service for Gabriel. Lastly, I need to get changed before we go to Kappa Kappa Werewolf. I'll be right back."

Before she could get out of the room Lex had stopped her. "You can't go back to work! Jesus, Nina! People are out to try and hurt you. You think some fucking daisies are more important than your life?"

Her eyebrows went so high at that comment that he knew immediately what a stupid thing he'd said. Cade got very quiet behind him.

"Let go," she said in a quiet, flat voice.

"I'm sorry, that didn't come out right."

"No, I think it came out just exactly right. Oh no, I'm not an architect, I don't own multiple businesses and wear watches worth more than my late-model sedan. Clearly my life's work—my shop—can't possibly be as important as what you do. Isn't that right, Lex?"

"Nina, I think your business is great. I'm not trying to belittle it. I just don't think flowers, or anything else for that matter, are more important than your life. You're my mate, I am biologically determined to want to protect you. And I quite happen to like you in one piece."

"There are three weddings and a business reception that I am contractually obligated to provide flowers for. These couples shouldn't have their wedding plans ruined because you people want to kill everyone in your sights! I have a business to run! It's a small business, I do well but if I just let it go I stand to lose everything. You grew up rich, you have no idea what it means to have built something like this on your own."

He could see the hurt in her eyes but the way she assumed that he was handed everything was hurtful, too. "I went to college to get my degree, Nina. I worked to become an architect. I work damned hard to protect Cade and this Pack. I wasn't handed anything. In fact, I have been trained since birth to be an Enforcer. It didn't matter that I may have had other plans. So I'm sorry that I said something insensitive but don't compound that by doing the same."

"Hey, you two. Come on. Nina, baby, we both love you and want you safe. But we understand you are a small business owner and we'll work out something to be sure you get your obligations taken care of. And Lex, you're taking what she said the wrong way too. I'm sure she knows how hard you work and the sacrifices you make every day. Let's not make things worse here. You love each other. Remember that." Cade put an arm around each one of them and leaned his head against theirs. He could feel the anger and the hurt drain out of each of them.

"I have to go change. Lex, I'm sorry if I hurt your feelings," Nina said softly, looking up into his face.

"I'm sorry too, gorgeous. I am proud of your business and like Cade said, we'll work something out. Go on and get changed, we'll be down here waiting."

She kissed Lex quickly and then tiptoed up to kiss Cade's chin and ran up the stairs to get dressed to go to the Pack house.

Lex turned to Cade and sighed. "Thanks."

Cade shrugged. "It won't be the last time you two will butt heads over her wanting to do something you think is dangerous or foolish. It's very clear she has a hot button about the whole class issue. You're both going to have to find a way to work through it and to figure out how to talk to each other without hurting the other."

Lex nodded. "Yeah. In the meantime, I'm putting guards on the shop and extra on you here too."

Cade had long since given up bristling at such measures. It was Lex's job after all.

* * * * *

Lex kept stealing looks at her. Really, the transformation was quite stunning. She had appealed to him as the buttoned up, pursed-lipped matron—but the Nina beside him blew his socks off.

Her long brown hair was gathered in a pretty clip thingy at the base of her neck and curls had escaped and framed her face in wisps. She didn't have a lot of makeup on, which was fine with him—he hated too much makeup. But what she did have was artfully applied. Her eyes looked huge and her lashes long. Those lips shimmered just enough to make him have to move around and adjust himself quite a bit. She was wearing a skirt that came to mid-calf and boots to go with it and she was one sexy woman in a red sweater.

She was every inch his mate and he thought she looked like a queen. When she became a wolf she'd be even more stunning. Pride radiated from his heart at how beautiful and strong she was but he also felt possessive of her. Putting an arm around her shoulders, he pulled her close and kissed her temple.

"What?" she murmured.

"You're beautiful. They're going to love you."

"Ha! Some of them maybe. But those girlfriends I keep bringing up—you know, the ones you keep changing the subject right after—I don't think they're gonna love me." She looked at him and narrowed her eyes. "But too bad, cause I don't share."

Cade chuckled from the backseat and Lex made a disgruntled snort of annoyance that only made Cade laugh harder.

They pulled up in the driveway of a large, colorful Victorian in Queen Anne and she made a low whistle. "This is really beautiful."

Lex got out and opened the door for them both, the guard standing discreetly but protectively at the ready. Cade brushed off his clothes and Nina watched as he pulled the mantle of leadership around himself, cloaking power at his shoulders. He was impressive before but this—she realized with a start—this was an Alpha.

Cade walked ahead of them up the grand porch that had really lovely furniture in small clusters from one end to the other. A glider swing, small tables, comfortable chairs and planters filled with seasonal greenery. Nina gave it a quick assessing look, critical. The plants needed some major attention. Hmph, she'd talk to Lex about it later.

The large double front doors opened up and a tall dark-haired woman stood there with a smile. "Alpha! Enforcer! It's been several days, I'm glad to see you. We were just ready to serve dinner."

Cade touched his hand to her cheek and she stepped back, her eyes lowered.

Lex urged Nina in after his brother and the tall woman looked up in surprise. "Oh! She bears your mark. Congratulations, Enforcer."

"Melissa, this is Nina Reyes, my mate. Nina, this is Melissa Warren, she's ranked fifth in the Pack."

Melissa looked at her with recognition. "Oh, you're Rey's sister. I'm so very sorry. I'm shamed that it was one of our own. Welcome to our Pack, although I do wish it was under happier circumstances."

Nina smiled. She felt that the other woman was genuine. She knew she was one of the suspects though and it wouldn't be wise to let her guard all the way down. "Thank you."

Cade took one of her hands and Lex held the other. They'd explained on the way over that everyone would know that Cade was her tri-bond and that in many ways, she'd hold a position much like his mate, even after he found his true mate she'd still have that connection to him and her place in the Pack.

As they walked through the long foyer deeper into the house, Nina took in all the details. The place was gorgeous. The details were authentic for the time period the house was built in. the colors, deep greens, deep wine and burgundy and creams and yellows, highlighted the furnishings and drapes. It was obvious that an interior designer had seen to all of those very important details. The wood gleamed, the banisters curved, the rugs were ornate and classic. The house was a masterpiece.

They walked through to a large dining room dominated by a large table. At their entrance, everyone in the room stood up.

Nina could feel the surprise ripple through the group as they took in the way that both men were holding her hands and she supposed they got her scent. She also couldn't help but be impressed at how everyone seemed to view Cade with deep respect and Lex with deep fear. She chuckled inwardly and thought about what a big pussycat he was deep down.

Cade stood at the head of the table, Lex and Nina to his right. "Everyone! We have had much sadness of late. Losing two of our own in such a short period of time. But there is reason to celebrate tonight. Lex, your Enforcer, has found and performed the Claiming with his mate. Better still, she is Nina Reyes, our Gabriel's sister. We have lost him, but she is here with us now."

The room got very quiet. Nina wasn't psychic but she could read people really well. She saw faces that were happy and faces that were not. She snorted inwardly when she noted that most of the unhappy faces were female. That didn't worry her as much as those faces she could not read at all.

She wanted to talk to Lex about it but she knew that their hearing was very sensitive and it would have to wait until they were out of there before she could bring it up.

"Well, let's eat shall we? And raise our glasses to Nina and Lex."

Nina saw Tracy there and grinned in her direction. She really did like her sister-in-law and she felt a bit more comfortable with a few friendly faces in the room.

Everyone in the room raised their glass and took a drink. A happy buzz of conversation filled the room once Cade nodded to Lex, who pulled out a chair for Nina, and they sat down.

Heaping platters of food were passed around and Nina watched with awe as they loaded their plates. Several of the Pack smiled at her, sending waves or tips of their glass in her direction.

Her eyes goggled when Lex tipped three pork chops onto her plate. "Whoa! One will do there, Hoss."

"You need to eat to keep your strength up. You've had a rough few days," Lex murmured and then frowned as she forked two of the chops back onto the platter and passed it to Cade.

"Lex, thank you for worrying about me but there's no way I can eat three pork chops. Hell, if I did that, I wouldn't have room for that pie I see over there." Nina tipped her head toward the sideboard that was heavy with desserts.

Melissa heard that and laughed. "Lex, you need to remember that humans don't have the same kind of metabolism that we do."

"Why on earth are we discussing humans at the dinner table? Don't ruin my appetite, please!"

The entire room's attention moved to the doorway where a blond man was standing in a very nice suit.

"Sorry I'm late, Alpha. I had to go to Issaquah earlier and traffic was nuts on I-90." He swept into the room.

Nina felt a wave of irritation bordering on rage and turned her head to see Cade stand up. He growled low in his throat. All the other wolves except Lex and the studly dude with the black hair across from her, Eric, lowered their heads and sat very still.

Nina's skin crawled with the power that rolled off Cade and that buffeted off Lex as well, who'd risen, shielding her with his body. Nina picked up her steak knife and held it, not knowing what was going on.

"Carter, would you like to apologize for that remark or choke on your teeth?" Lex said in a menacing tone and Nina stifled a squeak of fear as she thought she saw the flesh of his forearms ripple.

Cade, feeling her fear, put a hand on her shoulder and squeezed. "Stand down, Lex. Let me handle this," Cade said softly.

Lex remained standing and Nina peeked around his body and saw the blond looking up at Lex in confused terror. His eyes then moved to her and he jerked in surprise and he blushed furiously.

"Oh, man! I didn't know!" he stuttered.

Cade moved next to Lex. He turned and looked into Lex's face. "Alexander, I will handle this. Attend to your mate." Cade's voice was steel, his eyes unblinking and Lex let out a breath with a tremble and after several long moments, he sat down and turned to Nina, putting an arm around her shoulders.

Nina though, only had eyes for the exchange between Cade and the blond, even as she snuggled into Lex.

"Alpha, I apologize."

Cade looked at the other man without speaking. The tension in the room was thick as the moments ticked by.

"I'm waiting, Carter."

Carter? *Oh!* Blondie was one of the suspects and a bigot, too. Lovely. Well, Nina had to admit she'd had a few of her own ignorant thoughts about wolves herself. She made a mental note to really work on that.

Blondie nodded quickly and fell to his knees. He bent, forehead to the floor. "I apologize most sincerely for my ignorant remarks about humans."

Cade nodded once and looked down at Lex, who narrowed his eyes and then gave a very slight shrug.

"Get up, Carter and get some dinner. Then you can meet Alexander's mate, Nina. Rey's sister," Cade tossed this back over his shoulder as he turned and moved to his seat.

Carter's eyes widened as he stood up and looked at Nina. She couldn't tell if the shock was more than just, *oooh, shit I just talked smack about the boss' wife*, or her being Rey's sister or that he was guilty over something.

"I do apologize. It was stupid and insensitive of me," he said to Lex. Nina wondered if the reason he wasn't apologizing to her was another werewolf thing. Whatever the case, she didn't like this guy at all.

Lex nodded once and turned back to the table and everyone picked up their utensils and began to eat as the tension eased from the room.

Carter moved around the table and sat at Cade's left hand and looked down as he filled his plate.

"So, Nina, Rey said you own a flower shop?" Eric asked her smoothly.

Nina liked him for trying to ease the tension for her. "Yes, in Bellevue, as a matter of fact." She deftly blocked Lex's attempt to put three rolls on her plate, taking one and passing them on to Cade, who winked at her as he took the basket.

"Her shop is about three miles from the coffee shop," Lex said and frowned at her when she stabbed his hand with a fork when he tried to put another spoonful of potatoes on her plate.

Nina looked down the table. No less than four people rushed to ask her what she needed.

"Green vegetables? Salad?" Nina looked at the food laid out on the table.

They all looked at her blankly until Tracy laughed. "We'll have to lay in supplies of green vegetables for you. Wolves aren't much for salad."

"Oh my goodness! Let me run to the store," one of the wolves down at the far end of the table called out.

"No! It's okay, really." Nina held her hand up to stay her.

"Are you sure?" Cade asked.

"Of course. Sheesh, I was just looking for some green beans, I didn't mean to start anything." She barely held back her snarky comment but she didn't want to challenge his authority here with his Pack.

Lex kissed her temple. "We'll be sure to provide them for you next time."

She smiled at him and looked back to Eric. "So anyway, yes, I own a floral shop. I know Carter runs one coffee shop and Melissa the other, what do you do?"

"Oh, I help with the construction business. I do accounts payable and receivable and the ordering."

Carter steamed as he watched them all. He smiled and made nice but he couldn't believe he'd been made to prostrate himself like that before Cade—and over a human! She was pretty hot, though. He'd lay odds she'd be a tiger in the sack. Maybe he'd order the Rogues to subdue her so he could have a bit of quality time with her before he killed her.

That would be win-win for him because the grief, even with the tri-bond, would drag Lex down and he could be killed too, leaving Cade vulnerable. Maybe Carter would be running this Pack six months from now.

After they finished dinner, they got up and moved into the large living room where they mingled and Nina met the other Pack members who were there. It was nice that Tracy and Layla and Sid were there and their other sisters Megan and Tegan were part of the guard. It was a relief to have friendly faces that she knew were in her corner.

Lex kept looking toward the door until Nina finally rolled her eyes and sighed. "Jeez, what is it already? You keep looking at that door and it's working my last nerve."

"I need to go deal with something. Pack business. I'm going to get Megan over here before I do though."

Megan was part of Cade's guard but she was also being chatted up by a very cute wolf at the other end of the room. Nina put a hand out to stop him. "Oh for heaven's sake! I'm surrounded by your family, I'll be fine. I'll find someone to talk to." Which was part of their plan anyway.

He looked around and then back at her. "I'll be back in five minutes. Just don't leave this room."

"Okay, Dad. I won't run with scissors either."

He tried not to smile and failed. God, she was so totally irreverent. He dropped a kiss on her lips and left the room.

"You're a lucky girl," one of the women who'd had a not-so-friendly face on said as she sidled up to Nina. "You hit the jackpot with Lex."

"Yes, well. I think so." Nina smiled and resisted cracking on the cow, who was totally asking for it.

"He's very good in bed."

Nina smiled. "Yes, I know."

"This must be so awkward for you, being the only human here and all. Surrounded by people who all know your...man, better than you," Red said with a pout.

A laugh burst from Nina's lips. "Not as awkward as it must be for you. Honey, please. If you bent around any harder trying to let me know you fucked Lex to try and make me feel bad, you'd be a pretzel. Although you're about as smart as one."

Red's eyes narrowed and she moved in to try and menace Nina with her body. "Well! I was just trying to be friendly. It's not my fault Lex can't get enough women in his bed. He particularly likes the way I give head. I'm sure that it won't be a threat to your mate bond when he seeks me out. After all, you're only human. You can't possibly give him what he needs."

Nina didn't move an inch. "Look, Floozy McSkank, get the fuck out of my face or you'll find out just how well a human can defend herself," she said in a low voice.

Suddenly Tracy was at her side and Melissa on the other. "Cindy, you need to apologize for your behavior right now," Melissa said.

The room got silent again and Nina groaned and rolled her eyes. "It's fine. Ol' Floozy here was just about to move along. Right after I told her that if she ever so much as looked at Lex again I'd carve her eyes out with a plastic spoon."

Cindy's eyes widened and she took a step back and lowered her eyes. "I apologize."

Nina sighed and turned her back and saw Lex moving back into the room with alarming speed. "What is going on?" he demanded. "Are you all right?" He looked to Melissa and Tracy accusingly.

"She's fine, Lex. She held her own just fine." Tracy patted his arm and laughed as she and Melissa moved away. Frowning, he pulled Nina out into the hallway, away from the crowd.

"I was only gone for six minutes! Damn it, Nina! I shouldn't have left you alone."

"Lex, chill out or you'll pop a vein for god's sake. Everything is fine. It was a stupid girl thing. One of your chippies wanted to try and tell me you'd fucked her. As if that was news. You can't rush to my aid when stuff like that happens, it undermines me."

"Nina…"

She put her fingers over his lips. "Why don't you show me the rest of the house?"

He sighed and held his arm out and she took it. Once they were in the business office she shut the door and locked it. She moved to him and embraced him tightly, her lips going to his ear.

"We don't have time for that," he said teasingly as his hands went to her ass.

"Get over yourself. You have to leave me alone long enough to talk with people or this won't work," she said quietly into his ear.

He stiffened. "This is too dangerous. You saw how hostile Carter was earlier."

"That wasn't hostile, that was stupid. Anyway, we're in a house full of people, no one is going to hurt me. But I can't even start poking around if you won't leave me alone for two minutes. Go find Cade and leave me to mingle."

"Nina, you don't know werewolf culture very well. You would unwittingly offend or start something and it could go off the rails before you know it. You have to watch yourself and what you say. And Cade is...busy."

"Ahhh, gotcha. I thought I saw him making eyes at that chick with the cute jeans and pretty eyes." Nina pulled back and looked into his face. She twined her arms about his neck. "Well, I'd tell you to do what you normally do at these things but I have a feeling that involved you getting *busy* and since I'd have to kill you if you even thought about fucking another woman, I'll have to advise you to mingle or take a phone call instead. I'll be good. I promise not to start a war or anything."

He looked dubious but sighed because he knew she had her mind set on this stupid plan. "You have ten minutes, Nina, and I'm not leaving the room."

She tiptoed up and kissed his lips quickly. "Okay." Grinning, she bounded out of the room and he followed her out, glad she couldn't see him roll his eyes.

But Melissa only wanted to talk about where Nina got her boots and Eric was too busy staring at her breasts to say anything interesting. Nine minutes and fifty-eight seconds later, Lex showed up at her side and put his arm around her waist.

Carter came around then, slobbering all over Lex. "So wow, congratulations, Lex! Who'd have thought huh? Rey's sister? Under your nose all this time and everything."

He turned to Nina and gave her a look that was supposed to be pitying, but was really so artificial that she wanted to gag. "Welcome to the Pack, Nina. How come we've never seen you before? Were you and Rey close?"

Nina hated this asshole with the heat of ten thousand suns. How smarmy can you be? He was clearly fishing and using her dead brother to do it. "Rey and I were close in our own way. He came to me when he had a problem. But once he got bit he was very involved with Pack life and I had a business to run." She squeezed Lex's hand tight. "But I'm so glad he came to me at the end with that laptop."

Melissa's eyes lit with interest as Carter leaned forward. "Laptop? Do you mean you have something of Rey's? That could help find who killed him?" Carter said this, his voice filled with faux concern for Gabriel.

"We don't know what's on it but we hope so. He said some stuff, thought some answers were on the laptop. Oh, I suppose I shouldn't say anything else." Nina tried her best to sound clueless about the laptop.

Lex watched Eric's indolent posture change as Nina spun the story. He saw Melissa's interest and Carter's barely restrained curiosity.

"Well, I know a little bit about computers if you want help," Eric said, his eyes straying yet again to Nina's breasts.

"Will you excuse me a moment?" Nina asked them.

Lex looked down at her with alarm. "Are you all right?"

She shook her head at him and laughed. "Yes, I'm fine. I just need to go to the bathroom. I'll be right back. Stop being such a mother hen." She reached out and touched his face briefly and sauntered out.

Lex watched her until she turned the corner and had to ruthlessly hold himself in place to keep from following her. His mate was trouble and she invited it wherever she went but if he followed her to the bathroom, she'd kick his ass.

Instead he took his frustration out on Eric. "Pup, I appreciate the offer of help with the computer but if I ever catch you looking at my mate's breasts like that again, I'll rip your head from your body and beat you with your spine. Are we clear?"

Eric's blinked several times and he swallowed and dropped his gaze. "Yes, Enforcer."

Melissa laughed. "She's quite lovely, Lex. Strong. She'll be good for the Pack. Will she change soon?"

"That's for Nina to decide and not right now. She just lost a brother and her house was burned down by one of our own. You can't blame her for not trusting us completely," Cade said this with a bit of an edge in his voice as he came to stand next to Lex.

"So are you speaking for her now? I thought Lex was her mate." Carter wore a smirk as he spoke.

"I'm her Alpha and her anchor. That's enough."

"But he's not speaking for her, in any case, Carter. He's making a statement of fact." Lex glared at the other man. "She lost her brother. She's devastated and I'd never ask her to make such a big decision right now."

"Like being claimed?" Eric asked.

"You know that's just how it works, Eric," Melissa said with annoyance. "A mate is a mate. You can't change that. But becoming a new species, that's a big deal. Lex is right to wait."

"You think she'd want to change. It would make her stronger and faster, extend her lifespan. It would improve her in many ways," Eric said.

"God, what kind of pond scum was Rey, then? I mean, I know humans are bad but if being changed makes them better, he must have been one step below trash before he got bit."

"What did you just say?" Nina said, shoving her way through Cade and Lex and into Carter's face.

Lex moved closer trying to protect her. The room had gone silent and everyone was watching the exchange. "Honey, let me handle this," he murmured.

She turned and her eyes flashed at him with unshed tears. Her turmoil was clear in them, her guilt and rage. "Back off," she hissed and turned back to Carter.

"I...uh..."

"Yeah, that seems to be all you've got when someone confronts your bullshit attitude." She looked around the room. "You all feel the same way? That humans are scum? That my brother was trash?"

"Nina, honey," Cade said, an edge creeping into his voice. Things could go bad with a moment's notice with wolves and she was so damned fearless.

"Don't you Nina honey me! He said it right in front of you and you didn't say anything. My brother died for you people. He may not have been Mr. Upstanding Citizen, but he wasn't trash. From what I can tell, he ran your errands and took care of things for you so your hands didn't get dirty."

"I didn't say anything because you stormed in here before Lex or I could get a word out. You need to let me handle this," Cade warned and reached out but she stepped away and his eyebrows went up.

Nina turned back to Carter. "So, big man, say it. Or are you too much a coward to say it to my face? Huh?"

"Nina!" Lex said, grabbing her arm, pulling her back from Carter.

"Control your mate," Carter snarled and Nina broke free and was on Carter, knocking him to the ground. The heel of her hand was lodged against his windpipe, knees against his arms.

"Control this, you piece of shit!"

Lex pulled her off Carter, amazed at how fast and vicious she was for a human. He snarled at Carter, who was gasping for breath. Nina kicked and tried to break free.

"Put me down! Now, damn it!"

"Nina! Calm yourself. It's over. You proved your point," Cade said as she struggled in Lex's arms.

"I call a challenge!" Carter said as he got up.

The room erupted in a chorus of argument then.

"You'll stand down right now, Carter," Cade warned.

"She drew first blood. She disrespected my station. She's not a wolf, she doesn't have Lex's status. I use my right to challenge."

"If you do this, Carter, you'll be sorry," Lex growled.

"You bring this human into this house and she disrespects the Third and I'm supposed to be silent about it?"

"Carter, you started it. Come on, she's a human! She has no chance to defeat you," Melissa said urgently.

"Shut up or I'll challenge you after I kill her," Carter snarled.

Lex dropped Nina and lunged, grabbing Carter by the throat and backing him against a wall. "If I kill you first, it'll save us all the trouble."

"Lex! Stand down," Cade called out and Nina turned to face him, confusion on her face.

"You think I'm going to let this piece of shit kill my mate?" Lex asked, his voice less human than it had been just a moment before. His eyes had taken on a sort of luminous quality.

Tracy had moved to Nina's side and Megan, her sister-in-law who was one of Cade's guards, was on the other. The rest of Cade's guards were in the room, fanned out, waiting.

"You cannot interfere with a challenge! This is Pack territory. As Third, it's his right to challenge anyone who threatens his position. You would be subjecting yourself to censure and shunning if you interfere in that." Cade's voice was clear and unwavering but Nina felt his pain. Lex moved his hands away from Carter's throat but stayed close to him, effectively keeping his back to the wall.

Cade turned back to Nina. "But I'm sure that Carter understands how upsetting his comments were to Nina, who just lost her brother and to one of us. I'm sure that we can forget this whole stupid incident once everyone just calms down."

"I want this bitch's apology and I want her to show obeisance," Carter called out.

A collective gasp of outrage rippled through the room.

"Someone mind telling me what the fuck is going on?" Nina said.

"When you knocked Carter down in front of the Pack you showed him disrespect. And you nicked him and drew blood. As Third, it's his right to challenge anyone who is lower in rank than he is for such acts," Tracy murmured.

"Lower in rank? Challenge?"

"As a human, you don't have the same rank as your mate like you would if you were a werewolf. Essentially, you're a guest in the Pack, not a member of it. At least not in the sense that Lex is a member."

"Lovely. How equitable your society is. And this challenge is what? He wants to smack me around?"

Tracy paled. "No. Unless the challenger calls it off, a challenge is to the death."

"Are you kidding me? This asshole insults me, insults my brother and wants *me* to apologize or he'll use his genetically superior strength and speed to kill me?" She turned and looked back at Carter, body still hemmed in by Lex. "Very brave of him. I can see why he's so high up in the Pack."

Nina moved closer to Megan.

"I'll challenge him first. By challenging my mate, he's disrespected me," Lex called out.

"That's not how it works and you know it," Cade said. "You can challenge him...*after*."

Cade turned to Nina. "Honey, I know this is hard but if you apologize it'll all be over." His voice was hard but she could see the pleading in his eyes.

"Not just an apology, Cade. I want her obeisance, too," Carter called out.

"He wants you to apologize the way he did earlier," Megan said quietly.

"This asshat wants me on my knees kissing his shoes when he called my brother trash?"

"Nina, please," Lex begged, coming toward her. "Please, just apologize."

Pain knifed through her. "You two asked me to come here. You people, you changed my brother without his permission and then you killed him! This piece of shit insults my dead brother and all humans and *I'm* the one who has to apologize? What the fuck is wrong with this picture?"

"You can't win, damn it!" he hissed and grabbed her hands. "He is bigger and stronger and faster and he doesn't care about you. You can't beat him. Trust me to take care of this later but for now, please, apologize."

"Fuck you, Lex Warden. Fuck you and your stupid rules and this messed up assbackwards society where I'm a second-class citizen. Do you think I wanted any of this? I just wanted my damned shop and a bit of peace and you werewolves have stolen *everything* from me." She stepped back from him and looked at Cade and then the rest of the room. "I'd rather die than live without honor."

No sooner had the words come out of her mouth than Carter was on her, knocking her to the ground.

Her head hit the hardwood floor and she knew she was in big trouble. Still, she wasn't giving in without taking him down as far as she could. Carter was soft, she felt it in his hands and saw it in his walk.

His fist cocked and she rolled to the side and kicked back, hitting the back of his thigh, knocking him off and down.

"You bitch!" he screamed and his voice became a low growl.

"NO! You can't! She's not a wolf," Lex yelled. Four men were holding him back so he couldn't interfere with the fight—one of them was Cade.

Nina looked back toward Carter just in time for a sharp-clawed paw to strike her across her jaw, causing her to see stars. The metallic tang of blood exploded in her mouth and she spat it out, knowing from experience that if she swallowed it, she'd only get sick.

She got in a solid right hook and a heel to his balls and was able to stand. Blood dripped into her eye and she prayed she'd cut her head when she fell earlier. If he'd sliced her open with his nails, the chances of her getting the virus from him were higher.

Her ears rang from the next several strikes he made. Her left arm hung loosely at her side, broken. She could hear Lex screaming and howling. Others in the room were begging Carter to stop.

Carter punched her again until she finally went down. Just as quickly, he was on her and she felt his teeth pierce her neck. The shock of it gave her enough adrenaline to poke him hard in the eyes with her fingers and he backed off.

She broke free and he reached out and struck her and she flew back into Megan, who looked into her face, the helplessness and sorrow there was evident. Something caught Nina's eye as she fell to her knees.

Without thinking, Nina reached out and grabbed Megan's sidearm in her right hand and turned. With her good eye she sighted down her arm and pointed at Carter's head. The room got eerily silent for a moment.

"Shoot him!" Lex screamed, breaking the quiet. Choruses of "shoot him" broke out from the entire room.

"Should I shoot you, Carter? Maybe you should apologize to me. But I'll settle for you calling this fucked-up charade off. Now that I'm a wolf like you, I have status."

"Not yet, you don't," the half-wolf Carter growled out and lunged at her. Nina squeezed the trigger over and over until the chamber was empty and Carter was a heap on the floor.

"Who's sorry now?" she whispered and collapsed as chaos filled the room. The last thing she saw was Lex's anguished face as he picked her up.

Chapter Six

ဢ

Nina's eyes fluttered open. It was her bedroom, only different. The room was alive with detail. So much that she felt a bit overwhelmed with it all. Her heart pounded as she raised her head to look around.

"Nina! Oh thank god. You're awake."

She looked up into Lex's concerned face. "What the…? What happened?"

He put a covered cup with a straw in Nina's hands. "Here, drink this. I'm going to run into the hall and call the doctor. I'll be right back." Before she could question him again he dashed out.

Putting the straw in her mouth, she gagged as the taste hit her and set the cup down on the bedside table.

Lex yelled, "She's conscious!" As he came back into the room, Nina heard the echo of pounding feet running up the stairs.

He gave her an annoyed look when he came back in and sat next to her on the bed. "Why aren't you drinking that?" he barked sharply at her, putting the cup back into her hands.

She snorted. "Why don't you fuck off?"

"Ah, I see our girl is herself again," Cade said as he entered the room. Nina felt a rush of relief come from him. Relief and affection.

A tall, dark-haired woman came in and closed the door behind herself.

"Okay, is someone going to tell me what the hell is going on or what?" Nina repeated, losing patience.

"Didn't I just tell you to drink that?" Lex asked again.

"Didn't I just tell you to fuck off? This stuff tastes like ass. I'm not drinking it." She shoved the cup back at him but he refused to take it, his mouth set in a hard line.

"It's nasty, but really high in protein. You'll need it to help your body adjust." The woman smiled. "I'm Dr. Molinari. Welcome to Cascadia, Nina." She placed a satchel on the bed, pulled out a stethoscope and blood pressure cuff from it and moved to Nina's side, shooing Lex out of the way.

"Adjust? Doctor? If someone doesn't start explaining, I'm gonna get huffy."

"Yes, and god knows *that* would be a change," Lex said dryly from a safe distance. At the same time, Nina could feel the cool metal of his terror, only just barely gone.

"What do you remember?" Dr. Molinari asked as she took Nina's pulse.

"Uh, oh… I was jumped at the Pack house. I s-shot him. Jesus, I shot someone." The unreality of the events in that living room rushed back through her. The horror.

Cade moved to her side and tipped her chin up. "You had no choice."

"Did I kill him?" Nina whispered. Yes, she'd done it in self-defense, but she didn't want to be a killer.

"No. But close. You emptied the clip but it was lead ammo and not silver. Carter was high in the Pack, he's strong and has a great ability to heal."

"Does that mean he'll attack me again?"

"You won the challenge. Even though the challenge is to the death, he was so close that the governance council deemed it your victory." Cade smiled.

Rage flooded through her. "Oh, goody. Now that he's attacked me and made me into one of you while not a single fucking one of you did a thing to stop a werewolf from attacking a human—I'm victorious. Lucky me."

"I couldn't stop it, Nina," Cade's voice was filled with anguish. "As Alpha, I had to let the challenge go forward. You offended him. He had a rightful challenge. You could have apologized."

Nina sat up then and Lex moved forward to push her back to the pillows and she shoved at his hands. The Doctor tried to move Cade and Lex away.

"I could have apologized?" Nina shook her head. "It's my fault?"

"Nina, baby, Carter has been disciplined for biting you. We have rules about that. He's been stripped of his power and moved to the bottom of the Pack. Now that you're a wolf, you share my status as Second," Lex said softly.

"Oh you're all so civilized!" Nina said sarcastically. "You can attack a human in your living room as long as you kill her without biting her. With her husband standing three feet away!"

"You're upsetting her. It's hard enough on her wolf to have to heal this sort of damage to her system," Dr. Molinari told Cade and Lex with a frown.

"It's over now, Nina. You defeated him and you did it as a human. The rest of the Pack sees that as a mark of great power and they respect you for it."

She looked at Lex in disbelief. "Are you actually *proud* of that? Are you proud that I had to empty a gun into someone in your living room all over that twenty-thousand-dollar Oriental rug?"

"I'm proud that you were so strong—that you never gave up. Even standing there, your arm broken in three places, a gash on your head pouring blood, your throat nearly torn out—even then you fought back. Yes, I'm proud that my mate is so strong. More than that, I'm glad you're all right and safe." He knelt next to the bed.

"I need to be alone, please." Her voice was flat as she said it.

"You can nap. I'll just hold you," Lex said, touching her hand before she took it from him.

"Alone. As in, me only. I don't want to see another fucking werewolf." She looked straight ahead, not meeting anyone's eye.

"Nina, you're going to have to go through a change. You can't do it alone. The first time is very difficult," Dr. Molinari said soothingly.

"When?"

"Usually the first change comes at the full moon. After that you'll be able to change at will."

"The next full moon is?"

"In a week."

"Fine. Now all of you get the fuck out."

"Nina, why?" Cade asked softly, feeling both her and Lex's agony.

"Why what, Cade?" Nina turned to face him.

"Why are you sending us away?"

"You weren't there when I needed you. As in to live! You stood there while someone tried to kill me. I'm supposed to just take that with a smile?"

"Lex had to be restrained by nearly my entire guard! He almost risked Shunning to save you, Nina," Cade said, his voice hardening.

"*Almost* didn't save my life, Mr. Warden. In the end, all I have is myself. For a brief time, I allowed myself to think differently. Some lessons are apparently best learned the hard way."

"You allowed yourself to think differently? Mr. Warden? What the hell is wrong with you? What do you want, Nina? Blood?" Lex yelled.

Nina winced as his guilt, anger and fear rushed through their connection. "No. That's how *you* do it. All I want is for you to get out of my sight."

"Don't do this, Nina." Cade used his Alpha mojo on her and she felt herself begin to respond.

She gave an anguished cry and shot up out of bed.

"You need to lie down, Nina. I know you're upset but your system was just under attack from the virus and then your wolf healed all of that damage," Dr. Molinari said, reaching out to touch her.

"Nina!" Cade yelled so loud that the pressure of it knocked her to her knees.

She crawled toward the door and Lex picked her up and put her back in the bed. "Cade! Stop it," Lex said urgently.

"You can't keep me here." Nina huddled into a ball.

"The hell we can't! You're one of my wolves now, Nina. Mine to protect. You're not safe out there," Cade stated through clenched teeth.

"No, I'm not safe here. Nothing about you people is safe," she mumbled.

Dr. Molinari touched Nina's arm and then a sharp pain hit as the needle slid into her flesh and the heat of the sedative coursed through her.

"I can't believe you just did that," Nina slurred as her eyes slid up into the back of her head and she lost consciousness.

* * * * *

"Jesus, I can't believe how fucked up that was," Lex said, pushing a hand through his hair as he paced the hall outside their bedroom.

"She'll get over it." Cade slid down the wall and sat on the floor. Tracy put a mug of coffee into his hand and gave one to Lex as well.

"You have to let her deal with all of this, Lex. She's human. Or she was. She doesn't have a frame of reference for anything that's happened. She was changed, attacked, she doesn't feel safe. She expected you and Cade to protect her." Tracy held up a hand to stop them from arguing. "No, I'm not blaming you. I saw that it took four men to hold Lex back. I saw your palms bleeding where your nails pierced the skin, Cade. I know you did what you had to as Alpha. But she doesn't know that. She has no way of knowing. She'll see it. You just have to give her time."

Lex took his sister's hand and squeezed it. "Smart wolf." His anguish was clear in his voice.

"I'll help however I can. For what it's worth, Lex, she wouldn't be so upset if she didn't love you so much." Tracy cocked her head at her brother.

"There's more than just this," Cade said. "There's a lot of layers to that woman in there."

"It has to hinge on the past she's so stingy with. I've had my investigators on it for a month now. I think they should be able to come up with something soon. One way or another, Nina is going to share her past with me if it's the last thing I do."

"Lex, let her tell you. This whole situation is so tenuous, if you push her any further she's going to break," Tracy said gently.

"What about me?" Lex stood up with a yell. "Huh? You think I wanted this? You think I wanted a human mate who I fight with more than I make love to? She's a goddamned pain in the ass."

"Well, you know there are supposedly ways to undo the mate bond. Rumor of course, but I'm betting Grandma knows if they're true or not," Tracy said nonchalantly as she watched Lex.

"What? You think I'd dump her because she's difficult? I love that woman in there. I can't believe you'd try to get me to undo our bond."

Tracy rolled her eyes at him and Cade barked out a tired laugh.

"What are you laughing for?" Lex's face was angry until he got it. "Oh. Yeah. Okay, I got it, smarty-pants. But she should tell me. I shouldn't have to beg her to share her life with me."

"Lex, why are you so thick? She's obviously this way for a reason and the reason can't be very nice. We know that she and Rey were orphans and that she essentially raised him alone. Rey didn't share much more than that but from what I gathered, it wasn't pretty but she never let him down. She's got a spine of steel for a reason. You're both the most stubborn people I've ever met. You're made for each other and you know it and that's why you're both so prickly about it." With a smirk, Tracy grabbed the now empty mugs and went downstairs where other family members waited.

* * * * *

It was dark when Nina awoke from her drugged sleep. She knew immediately that Lex was in the room, sleeping next to her in their bed. She lay there for a long time thinking about the whole situation, not knowing what to do.

She loved Lex Warden and there was no denying the connection between them. At the same time, she couldn't get around the terror and betrayal she'd experienced as Cade stood there doing nothing. Yes Lex had to be restrained but he had a gun, she knew that. Why hadn't he just shot Carter? She'd have done it for him. Hell, she'd had to do it for herself and that's what burned deep in her gut.

She'd been forced to put herself and her life in the hands of these two men. It hadn't been easy but she'd done it. When she'd entered the Pack house that night, she hadn't thought for a moment that she'd be unsafe. No, she'd felt the deep comfort of belonging. The ease of partnership instead of the pressure to be in charge—not always having to guard and protect. Those few hours had been perfect and the comparison between then and what she felt as she stood there while they all watched someone try to kill her sliced through her heart and left her in tatters.

And she had no idea what to do about it.

"How are you feeling?" Lex asked quietly, not moving from her side. He somehow knew she was awake.

"Like a werewolf tried to kill me."

"Nina, I'm sorry. I'm sorry I hurt you. Sorry you lost faith in me—in us."

"I don't know what to say, Lex. They're nice words and I'm sure you actually mean them. But this is just one more in a long line of fuckups in my life and I'm so tired."

"Please tell me. Help me understand, Nina. I swear to you I'll do the same. We can't go on this way. We need to try and know each other if we are going to make this work. And I want to. I love you."

She thought about it. Could she do it? Could she expose herself and tell him her story after what had happened? Could she trust him? Because if she didn't open up, she wasn't sure they'd make it. But he was Mr. Law and Order, what if she was repulsed by what she told him? What if he couldn't accept her past?

She'd held on to her secrets for a very long time, never letting anyone in. She wasn't sure she'd even lived really. She had a house and her shop but never really any true interaction—intimacy—with anyone. When you opened up, you took risks that what you shared could be used to hurt you. And that terrified her. But losing Lex terrified her more.

Reaching down, she opened the door she'd kept barricaded for so long. "About three weeks after my twelfth birthday my parents went off on a trip. It was just for three days. My daddy was going to bring me back saltwater taffy from the shore.

"Gabriel and I were playing in the yard of some family friends and the police came. They told us that my parents had been killed in a fire at the hotel. A lot of stuff happened, I don't remember all of it but eventually they put us with a distant cousin of my mother's. But they hated us. They just liked the money.

"And Gabriel was...he didn't know how to deal with our parents being gone. He'd been such a sweet child but he got in with the wrong crowd and got in trouble. A lot. Before long they'd kicked us out."

Nina relayed the story in a quiet voice. Lex reached out slowly and took her hand, relaxing when she didn't pull away.

"What did you do?"

"They wanted to put us in foster care but they couldn't guarantee that we'd stay together and even at just ten, Gabriel was already on track for trouble. I couldn't take the chance of being separated from him. So we ran. I was nearly fifteen and I worked odd jobs and we lived here and there, ducking the social workers and the system. I became an expert at lying to get what we needed.

"First I ran street cons with some other, older kids. But then I ran up against the small time hoods who were part of organized crime. I was a pickpocket. I stole food. I stole clothes. I stole things I could resell for money to pay for rent. I got picked up a few times. Did a few stints in juvie.

"I cleaned houses for a while. I think one lady I worked for knew we were on the edge, saw how desperate I was. She helped me get into some continuing education classes and I got interested in computers. She had one and let me use it. I started keeping her books for her. I don't know where I'd be today if it weren't for her."

Nina began to cough. Her throat was so dry. Lex sat up quickly and poured a glass of water, handing it to her in the cool darkness of the room. A few minutes later she stacked pillows up and sat against the headboard.

"Anyway, the money was all right. She let us live in an apartment over the garage. Gabriel was nearing eighteen and I was so afraid he'd end up in jail. I started hacking for fun. It was a way to pass the time as I waited up for him to get home. And I got to be good. Really good.

"People found me and hired me to do jobs for them. I never hurt anyone but I broke the law, Lex. I used the money on hospital bills. Damn Gabriel was always getting in fights, needing stitches or bones set and casted.

"But there were crackdowns and I was terrified of getting caught. If I went to prison what would happen to Gabriel? I wanted to have enough money to walk away. To get us across the country and set us up. So I did one last job. I nearly got caught but it netted me a very, very large payoff.

"I bought two bus tickets and picked Gabriel up and we traveled for a few days and ended up here. We lived in an apartment and I got my GED and went to community college and discovered how much I loved floral design and plants and flowers in general. I was good at the business side of things but I was always careful to not have a computer at home hooked up to the internet.

"We'd gotten out. I had a business and things were good. And then Gabriel got bitten in that bar fight and I couldn't protect him anymore. He was your problem and god help me, I was relieved. I loved Gabriel but twelve is too young to be a mother."

Lex's heart was pounding as he listened. He ached for her. He'd told her that he hadn't been handed anything—and he hadn't, he'd worked hard for his accomplishments—but compared to her life, he'd had it so easy.

"People have failed me my entire life, Lex. The only constant I've had was myself. I'm not proud of the things I've done. I know they were wrong. But it was all I knew how to do. Maybe I should have let us go into foster care. I don't know. All I had was myself." Her voice broke as she repeated it.

"I believed in you. I allowed myself to believe that for once in my fucking life I was with someone who might take care of me every once in a while. Or at the very least, take care of themselves so I wouldn't have to."

Her entire body began to tremble at the effort to free all of the things she'd kept inside. "I trusted you. I trusted Cade. I don't know how to get back from this place where I feel so betrayed."

Lex leaned over her and turned on the lamp, casting a low golden light into the room. He sat next to her, searching her face.

"Oh, baby. My poor wounded bird." He kissed her fingertips and realized he could scent her wolf and he had to close his eyes for a moment as the intensity of the feeling passed through him.

"Why, Lex? Why would you all stand there and watch someone kill me? You don't think issuing a challenge to the death was a bit of an overreaction for a nick on the forehead? Could you really just watch as he killed me, Lex? You had a gun, you could have shot him first. Do I really mean so little that an entire room of people would do nothing to stop him from killing me?" Nina's voice was a mere whisper, laden with emotional turmoil.

Lex took a deep breath. "Werewolves have existed, hidden from humans, for thousands of years. We've only just come out in the last hundred years. All that's kept us safe, free from persecution and being hunted to extinction, was the Pack.

"The Pack is life, Nina. Our rules create order. A Pack is a unit. You have to trust everyone in that unit to get your back if you're attacked. Our rules aren't just words and ceremony—they're wired into our very existence.

"You felt it when Cade spoke earlier, I know you did. It's biological determinism for werewolves. But in order for a hierarchy to exist unchallenged—to avoid infighting and backstabbing—every wolf has to rely on the absolute of the rules that govern us.

"We can't obey the rules only when it suits us. If Cade had stopped the challenge, the Pack would have torn him apart. Literally. They would have lost confidence in his leadership. That would have thrown the Pack into total chaos.

"Cade was born to lead this Pack. Just as I was born to be the Enforcer. It's my job to enforce our laws." His voice hitched with deep emotion. "I would have killed Carter if he'd killed you. But they took my guns, I couldn't have shot him. Challenge or no, I would have ripped him apart with my bare hands and then I'd have withered away without you."

Tears were running down her face and he reached out and took the teardrops with the tips of his fingers. They clung there like diamonds. He put them to his lips—taking her inside of him.

"I'm sorry that I couldn't be what you needed. I'm not making excuses for it. Carter betrayed the Pack by misusing his position. It's one reason why the rest were so quick to demote him so severely. But Cade couldn't have stepped in. He had to weigh your life against the existence of the Pack he was born to protect. It wasn't easy for him, but there was no other choice."

She looked into his face for several long minutes. She didn't speak, she just studied his features as she drank him in. Aside from being incredibly handsome, there was something about the shape of his eyes, the curve of his bottom lip, the fuzz of his day-old beard—something about the sight of him that calmed her.

She reached out and touched his bottom lip and they both shivered at the contact. So much existed between them that there weren't words adequate to express it all. Love and hope, hurt and anger, disapproval and betrayal, but above all, connection. Love is not simple, it is not easy. But between them, it simply existed.

It was like slow motion as Lex brought a hand up to enfold her hand in his larger one. "You're still recovering. We should wait."

Her eyes narrowed and he laughed. She shook her head. "I need a shower."

"Dr. Molinari said that would be fine. Do you need help?" He got up gingerly. His cock was so hard it ached. His wolf was barely leashed, wanting to mark her, excited that she now had a wolf. It took their bond to a completely new level. Where before he'd been able to keep his wolf suppressed because Nina was human, there were no such restraints now and his wolf knew it.

He walked into their bathroom and turned on the water to let it run and get it warm. His back was turned but he felt when she walked into the room. Not just with his more sensitive hearing and sense of smell, but deep inside.

Turning, he caught her eye and their wolves caught scent of each other.

Her eyes widened as her breathing quickened. "What is that?" Her hand gripped the bathroom counter.

"Our wolves. They scented each other." He moved to her and pulled her shirt off, tossing it in the hamper, and then shoved her panties down. One of her hands rested on his shoulder as she stepped out of them, kicking them aside.

He groaned and her hand tightened. "Lex," she said in a purr.

"No. Don't tempt me, Nina. You need a shower and then you need to get back in bed. You were so hurt..." His voice broke and he turned quickly, opening the shower enclosure and she sashayed in.

The warm water sluicing down her body felt really good and she sighed at the pleasure.

"Tease."

"Shut up about that. It's my job to be desirable. But you can tell me why I don't seem to have any actual symptoms from my fight with Carter except for some muscle soreness and fatigue."

He chuckled. "The change did it. We heal very quickly. You were out for two days and while you were unconscious your wolf healed your body."

"You should come in here. I'm having a hard time reaching my back. Plus, I can't really hear you."

Lex rolled his eyes but that didn't stop him from stripping off his clothes in record time and getting into the enclosure with her.

"Here." She handed him the soap and a washcloth and turned around.

He cleaned her back and tried not to think about how alluring she looked there, wet and glistening. Her scent rose on the steamy air and tempted his senses.

"So, you were saying that my wolf healed me? And okay, so you have to explain this a bit. I have a wolf? I mean, am I not a werewolf? It's separate? And Gabriel was in the hospital for four days after he was bitten, he barely made it."

"It's difficult to explain but yes, you have a wolf. When you're in human form it sort of curls up inside of you. It's metaphysical stuff, I can't do it justice. But it's a part of you."

She turned and tipped her head back, rinsing her hair. Her back arched and brought her into contact with his body and his body tightened.

"And uh," he cleared his throat, "Rey wasn't as strong as you are. I'm sorry, I realize that sounds cold, but it's the truth and the reason why your body dealt with the conversion so quickly and healed so fast."

She reached back and squeezed the water from her hair as she moved aside. "You want in here? I'll scrub your back since you were so helpful." She quirked up a saucy smile and he laughed.

"I'm good. I showered before I came to bed." He stepped out and handed her a towel.

"Oh my! It's warm. Did you just get it from the dryer or something?" She wrapped her hair and he gently patted her back and legs dry.

"The towel bars are heated, like the floors." He was on his knees as he finished drying her legs. He looked up her body and caught her staring, lips parted, breath quickened.

"Uh, wow. Nice. The architect must be a smart guy who likes comfort." An eyebrow went up.

"Well, he had no idea he'd have a beautiful mate to keep warm, but he's glad he thought of it."

"Okay, let's stop talking in the third person now. Instead, I propose that you fuck me." She ran her fingers through his hair and pulled him closer to her body.

"Nina…"

"Oh what now?"

"You're still healing. We should wait." Unable to help himself, he leaned in and inhaled, the rich scent of her body.

"Gah! You with the talking. Shut up and fuck me already! Your little mister certainly wants to."

He stood and pushed her back into the bedroom with his body. "My what?" His voice was incredulous.

"Thingy. Wee-wee. Johnson. Hoo-hoo. You know," she indicated his cock, "that."

Barely holding back a laugh, he bent, grabbing and picking her up. He placed her on the bed gently. "How old are you, Nina?" He scrambled up after her, leaning over her body but keeping his weight on his elbows instead of on her.

"I'm thirty and yes, it's weird for me to actually say *cock*. I can say it in my head, but it's weird to say it out loud."

"What did you call it before?"

"What do you mean?"

He actually growled and she arched a brow.

"With the *others*. I have a hard time understanding a man who would be fine with you referring to his cock as his little mister."

She burst out laughing. "Oh Scooby, is this about my saying 'little' before the mister part?"

"Partially. And did you just refer to me as a cartoon dog?" He wandered off as he realized what she'd said and then remembered she had dodged him. Clever wolf, his mate. "Answer my question."

She blushed fiercely. "I...you know there haven't been many men before you. I didn't call it anything, I don't think. And it's not little. You know that."

He kissed her quick and hard. "Big huh?" He smirked. "Oh. Good. I look forward to you saying it to me. A lot."

"Well are you gonna do anything with it or talk us both to sleep?"

"Well first, let's get your pussy ready for me." He slid down her body, parting her thighs as he went.

"Yes, okay," she replied faintly. "You know the wolves are all about the oral sex, it's a bonus in favor of the whole conversion thing. I don't think it comes standard with other types of convers...omigod!" She gasped as the tip of his tongue slid against her.

Slow, long licks of his tongue drew her toward orgasm. The sinuous slide of the flat of his tongue was heaven. He lapped with more pressure as he drew up and over her clit, pressing against it, pressing it against her body. The sensation made her breathless and tingly and altogether wonderful.

The emotional nature of their conversation, and really of the last weeks, rushed through her. She could feel the intensity of his feelings for her, could feel how much he loved and desired her.

When he slid one finger and then two deep into her pussy and stroked over her sweet spot in time with suckling her clit, her back arched and she couldn't help the long moan of his name that escaped her lips as orgasm slammed into her body.

His mouth on her brought gentle love but the climax was spectacular in force. It was vivid and spine bending and it seemed to echo through her body for long minutes until she finally collapsed, muscles utterly relaxed.

Dimly, she heard his superior male chuckle as he settled in next to her and put his face in her neck to breathe her in.

"That was pretty spectacular, studly," she managed to gasp out.

She didn't need to open her eyes to know he was wearing that smug smile of his and she allowed it because he deserved it.

"If they ever have an Olympic sport in oral sex, you would totally win the gold."

"Why thank you. But I think my professional days are over and I'm retired now. There's only one subject that interests me and I plan to perfect my technique between her thighs."

She snickered. "Well, yeah. Jeez. No one meant that you'd go off and ply your trade on other chicks. Not and remain living."

He stroked his fingertips over her stomach and she cracked an eye open and turned her head to look at him.

"I hope you're not thinking I'm doing the work and being on top. I was just nearly killed and all."

"Nina, beautiful, let's just rest. Go to sleep."

She rolled over onto her side to face him and frowned. "Don't you want me?"

"Oh god, yes! Of course I do. All day long. Every moment of the day. But you're recovering from traumatic injuries, I can't! It would be taking advantage."

Nina blinked at him. "Are you fucking kidding me? Look, Dr. Phil, shut up already and fuck me. I'm not saying I'm up to sixteen pages of the Kama Sutra or anything, but I can most assuredly handle a nice bit of slap and tickle."

"Sweetheart, you're my mate. It's my job to protect you."

With a sigh she reached down and grabbed his cock. It was so hard that she felt it throb in her hand. The head glistened with pre-cum. She slid her thumb up and over, through that silky slickness and brought it to her lips. He groaned.

"If you don't fuck me, I'll go insane. That's how you can take care of me, Scooby. Come on, give me some of that magic semen of yours," she teased.

He rolled his hips, thrusting himself into her hand. "Come on. I promise that I'll nap afterward. You know you want to. If you don't, I'll tell all the other wolves you don't satisfy my naughty, dirty, filthy, unspeakable urges."

"God, you're one of a kind. You know that?" Lex laughed as he extricated himself from her hand and gently pushed her back onto the bed.

"Well, of course," she replied, breathless with anticipation.

He didn't disappoint as he lined himself true and nudged himself into her pussy. Both of them closed eyes for a moment as he made an inexorable push into her body with his own.

Beads of sweat lined his forehead and his spine as the molten, wet silk of her pussy parted for him. She hugged him, welcomed him. When he hilted it felt like home. Had anything ever felt this way? Good and right—the way you feel when you come back from a long vacation?

He kept most of his weight off her body, taking it on his arms. She rolled her hips up to meet his thrusts and she opened more fully when she wrapped her legs about his waist. She used her calves to pull him deeper and hold him there.

"You feel so good, Lex. Nothing has ever felt this good." She whispered the words as she stared deep into his eyes.

He felt the catch of her emotions and heard it in her voice. He knew then that she'd never laid herself bare emotionally like that to anyone before. That humbled him, made him realize just how special she was, crunchy exterior and all.

"That's because it is good, beautiful. You and me? We're it."

"Sweet talker," she said, ending on a gasp as he held her hips so that he could change his angle, stroking the fat head of his cock over that bundle of nerves deep inside her.

"Yeah, I still got it."

"Okay, Lassie, less talking, more fucking."

"God, you're a test on a man," he sighed and she laughed. He realized that he'd heard her snicker and giggle and even chuckle but never a full out laugh. Not like this one, full of joy and free of hesitance and pain.

"I love you, studly," she said in a rush and her eyes widened in shock.

"Hey, I love you too. Don't be afraid to love me, Nina. I hope I never make you regret it." He looked into her face and then blushed. "Oh, well, except for the whole last month or so." He kissed her. Her lips were gentle and full beneath his. He sipped at her.

"Touch yourself, Nina. Make yourself come around me. I don't want to put any of my weight on you to move my hand. And I like to watch you do it."

He leaned down and ran the edge of his teeth over one of her nipples, delighting in the way she mewled and arched into his mouth. Watching her hand slide over her mound, fingers questing toward her clit, he flicked his tongue over her nipples, one and then the other, over and over.

The moment her fingers touched herself she tightened around his cock. He could feel the flesh of her pussy slide around as she moved her fingers over herself. Her breath quickened and caught as she pushed herself toward orgasm with him right behind her.

He loved the way she felt beneath him, around him. Loved the subtle scent of her body that rose from her heated skin. Loved the way her hair felt against his skin, the silk of her inner thighs. Loved the sounds she made as she neared climax. Hell, he even loved her twisted sense of humor.

As the first tremors of her orgasm rippled through her cunt, he began to thrust deeper. Fighting the urge to plunge deeply into her, he settled for slow, deep digs into her and when it broke over her the spasms and slickness of her climax yanked him in with her and he thought his insides would shoot out the head of his cock, he came so hard.

Panting, he moved to the side so he wouldn't collapse on her and hurt her. Heart thundering in his chest, he pulled her to him, kissed the top of her head and murmured that he loved her.

Chapter Seven

ଇ

As dawn broke, Nina's internal alarm clock woke her for the first time since she'd moved into werewolf mansion. She got out of bed and jumped into the shower quietly. She had to get back to work. She'd managed to get out of Lex that they'd at least called the shop and arranged for her manager to take over while she was gone, but enough was enough. It had been a week and that was too damned long.

She did enjoy the fact that the master closet was off the bathroom and got dressed, dabbed on a bit of makeup and twisted her hair up. She decided to forego the glasses and the prim clothes. They'd burned anyway. What was the point now that she not only had a man but a big bad werewolf who carried a .357 Magnum?

She left Lex sleeping and headed down and thankfully smelled coffee and saw Dave and Megan there in the kitchen, reading the paper.

The truth was, she understood better than Lex thought she would. She understood the importance of sticking to rules to be safe. Understood the cost of taking care of a larger goal — sometimes at the expense of the weakest person.

At the same time, she wasn't sure how she felt about the rest of the wolves who stood there and watched while she was nearly killed. Her logical mind understood it — certainly understood the compulsion of Pack now that it coursed through her veins. It was like an odd sort of hive-mind, *or was that Pack-mind?* connection. Still, the feelings of betrayal were still there like a bitter taste on her tongue and weighed heavy on her heart.

But she lived there and now she was one of them in more than just marriage. And she couldn't avoid them all forever.

Sighing, she walked into the kitchen and headed for the cabinet to grab a mug.

Dave jumped up and opened the door, pulling a cup out and handing it to her. "Here, let me help you with that."

Nina took it from him. "Thanks." She turned and got milk from the fridge and made her cup of coffee.

She popped a bagel in the toaster, rustled through the refrigerator and pulled out a tomato and some cheese and set to slicing them.

"Nina, I'm sorry. I know you probably can't understand why no one helped you and I...I'm so terribly sorry," Megan said softly.

Nina turned and looked into her sister-in-law's eyes and she felt the pain there. Felt the conflict between her loyalty to the Pack, to her Alpha and to doing the right thing and protecting Nina.

But as Nina stood there, remembering that night she had a flash of something. The guards all carried weapons, yes. But they also carried them strapped in thigh holsters, at the small of their backs or underarm holsters. Nina looked down and saw that Megan's gun was not on her thigh.

"Megan, where do you carry?"

Her sister-in-law moved her jacket back and showed Nina the underarm rig. "Here. Sometimes on the thigh but not most of the time."

"Not most of the time." Nina said this quietly and Megan made a barely perceptible nod. Nina closed her eyes for a moment. *Certainly not that night at the Pack house.* Nina remembered Megan adjusting herself as they got out of the cars before they'd walked into the house.

Megan had handed her that gun. Had used that moment of confusion when Nina had been thrown into her to get that gun into her hand.

Nina reached up and touched Megan's face gently. "Thank you." Understanding passed between them.

"I wish you'd gotten my gun. I was carrying silver ammo and you would have killed that bastard, Carter." Dave's voice was vehement.

Nina turned to Dave with a shrug. Dave looked miserable, guilty and red-faced.

"I'm sorry, too. I'm glad you shot his ass. I hope it hurt like a motherfucker to get those slugs out of him. I hope Doc Molinari dug in extra hard to get them all. Can you forgive us all?"

"I'm working on it. It'll be a while before I'll be ready to deal with the Pack as a whole again."

Her bagel popped up and she turned, piled it with tomato slices and cheese and took it to the table.

"You're going to need some more protein to go with it," Cade said as he came into the room and went to the fridge. He pulled out some roast beef, put it on the table in front of her and went to get himself some coffee.

Suddenly Megan and Dave found that they had things to do in the other room as Cade sat at the table across from Nina.

She said nothing as she put meat on the bagel but she could feel his anguish. And his irritation and confusion at wanting her approval and forgiveness. She softened a bit, but not much. She'd wager that he'd never actually had to work for anyone's approval before as he'd been groomed to be Alpha from the womb and all.

"So. Am I still Mr. Warden?" Cade asked, watching her as she sipped her coffee.

"I don't know. Are you?"

"What kind of woman answer is that?"

"What kind of stupid-assed question is that?"

"Did you just call me stupid?"

"No, I called your question stupid. But upon reflection, I should have included you, too. But, as you're the supreme poobah, you can be the *most* stupid."

"Look, I don't apologize for doing what was necessary to keep Pack order."

"How furry of you to say so." She got up and went back to the fridge. Annoyed, she pulled out eggs and milk, placing them on the counter.

Nina could feel Cade glaring at her back as she pulled out a bowl and a whisk and set about making scrambled eggs. She took her time just to fuck with him.

"We can't just keep being mad at each other, Nina. You're my sister-in-law and I'm your anchor bond as well as your Alpha."

She turned on the gas below the skillet and put a pat of butter in to melt. "Hmm. Is that an official pronouncement?"

She tipped the bowl, pouring the mixture into the skillet, and put it in the sink before moving back to the stove where she stirred the eggs.

He fumed as the food cooked. Finally she pulled out two plates and halved the eggs and put one plate in front of Cade and sat down with hers.

"Oh. Thanks."

Nina hid a smirk at his confusion. Cade Warden might be her Alpha and the big cheese, but he and his tool of a brother had to be properly trained as to how to treat a woman. This He-Man routine of theirs had to stop. If she was going to live there, it would be on her terms, too, or not at all.

They ate in silence until she stood up and put her plate in the sink.

"So are we okay or what?" Cade asked.

She turned to him. "Eventually I think we will be. On one level, I trust you. As a member of your Pack, I trust you'll enforce the rules that keep werewolves safe. But that doesn't mean I trust you, Cade, to protect me, Nina. I would have given my life for you or Lex. But you don't feel the same and that's taking some getting used to."

He stood and went to her. Taking her hands in his, he searched her face as he tried to think of the words to say. "Nina, you can trust me. There is no one more important to me in the world than you and Lex. I love my family but you two are my tri-bond. In many ways, you're my mate too. It nearly killed me to watch you being attacked. I tried to find you a way out. And no, I don't think it was your fault. But I also knew that a werewolf could easily kill a human. I had to make the choice that was best for the Pack. But that doesn't mean you can't trust me."

"You can't have it both ways, Cade." She gently took her hands back and kissed his cheek. "I'll get over it in time. But I don't think things between us will ever be the same and maybe that's a good thing anyway."

"What are you doing up so early?" Lex asked as he came into the kitchen.

Nina stepped away from Cade and went to Lex. She kissed his chin. "I have to get to my shop today. It's been a week. I'll need a car. Oh, and I suppose a bodyguard, too." She sighed.

"You what? Jesus, Nina! You. Almost. Died! People are trying to kill you. They burned down your house. What does it take to make you stay home and be safe?" Lex yelled this so loud that the bass of it vibrated her spine.

She idly waved a hand in his direction. "Indoor voice! Knock it off tantrum-boy."

"Tantrum-boy? Nina, Lex is right. You need to stay here where we can protect you."

She narrowed her eyes at Cade. "Oh yeah, well, let me see…nope, you're not the boss of me. And I'd like to point out a very important point—this entire ball of shit originated with werewolves. The murder attempts? You people. Hell, right in front of you in one situation. So, fuck off, won't you? Because I've got a business to run and we still need to find my brother's killer."

She moved to walk out of the room and Lex's arm shot out to stop her. Only she turned and growled at him and everyone got very quiet for a moment.

"Nina, your wolf is surfacing." Cade's voice was calm and low.

"Don't poke at it with a stick, then." She turned back to Lex. "I'm going to work. Period. End of discussion. I'm going to wait downstairs for five minutes and then I'm taking one of the Mercs and leaving. You can roll with that and give me a bodyguard. Or sit here and wring your hands all day. It's all the same to me."

With that pronouncement, she breezed out of the room.

Lex slammed a fist into the wall and let out a frustrated groan. "Are you in the field today or here?"

"Here. Go with her, Lex and take Megan with you. It's time you let Dave take over being my chief bodyguard and you do Enforcement full time. Right now, she's our biggest priority. She's under threat and she's right, we do need to find that murderer."

"Carter is a part of it. I can taste it."

"I think so, too. I've never doubted your senses about stuff like this anyway."

Lex sighed and turned to his brother. "I'm going to bring two more men onto your personal detail."

"Do it. Now get down there before she takes off without you."

Lex grinned and held up a small black cube. "Not without the electronic key she doesn't. The engine won't turn over without it."

Cade laughed. "Living with the two of you is going to be really interesting."

"Something like that," Lex called out as he left the room. He motioned for Megan to follow him and they headed downstairs to the garage.

* * * * *

Nina was sitting in the car, talking on her cell phone when they got inside with her. She shot him an annoyed look when he touched the cube to a spot on the dash near the ignition and started the car. He made sure she saw him pocket the cube where he could keep custody of it, too.

"Who were you talking to?"

"My assistant manager. He's going to Pike Place Market this morning to pick up some supplies and…oh, not like you need to know the details."

"Yeah. Well, here's how it's going to go." Lex kept his eyes on the road as he drove. "One of us, more probably, two of us, will be with you at all times while you are at the shop. I will drive you daily. This is not negotiable. You will not leave the shop without one of us accompanying you. You will not enter the shop until we have done a sweep and ensured everything is clear."

"Yeah, yeah. Okay, Principal McGruff."

Megan snorted laughter in the backseat and Lex cut his eyes to her in the rearview mirror but she studiously avoided looking up.

"I mean it, Nina. Now that we're mated it's going to be even more difficult for me to let go of you. I'll be more protective. It's biology. If we work together, we can make it easier. Come on, you seriously can't…oh shit!"

Nina's head came up and she saw the smoking ruin of her shop. Automatically her hand went for the door but Lex was quicker, hitting the automatic locks.

"No! Nina, I know you're upset but you can't charge out there." Megan leaned forward and rubbed Nina's shoulders, murmuring softly to her.

"I have to talk to the police." Nina's voice was flat. "Pull over here, there are plenty here now."

Lex started to argue but met his sister's eyes. Megan shook her head once, staying his actions. With a sigh, he pulled over in the parking lot of the bookstore next to the shop.

"Stay here until I get your door." Lex slid out and surveyed the area as he walked around to let her out of the car.

He led her to the firefighters on scene, trying to stifle his alarm at how limp and lifeless she felt as she let him lead her around.

"Officers, my fiancée, Nina Reyes is the owner of this shop. What's happened?" Lex asked as they got to the police line.

"Ma'am," one of the firefighters said as he pulled off some of his smoke-stained gear, "it doesn't look accidental."

"Arson? Oh, of course! Because it wasn't enough to burn down my house. Oh! Everyone is okay? Oh god! There was no one here yet? You see, for early deliveries on Thursdays, we're often here at five. None of my employees was ins…" her voice broke and Lex pulled her to his side.

Megan stood discreet but alert at their back.

"No ma'am, the place was empty. Can you wait over there please?" The firefighter pointed at the corner. "I'm sure the police and the investigators will want to talk to you."

Numb, Nina let Lex guide her to the corner to wait. She had to let the grief wash over her so she could get to the mad. Instinctively, she knew the mad would save her, help her get through.

Lex stood next to her, rubbing small circles over her back. She'd noticed that the wolves liked to touch at times of stress. She also realized that she'd have to stop thinking of it as things that happened to *them* because she was one of them too.

"When this is all over, I'm going to check myself into a hospital and have a heart attack," she said tiredly.

"I'm so sorry, beautiful. We're going to find who did this, I promise you."

"Carter did this, Lex. Come on! You know it and I know it," she hissed as she saw someone come over from the scene. It was the man who was investigating the fire at her house.

"Ms. Reyes. I wish I could say I was happy to see you. Do you happen to know anything about this?" Detective Stoner came to a stop in front of them.

"I wish I did. I was coming to my shop for the first time in a week." Nina felt the anger and the frustration at not being able to tell this man the whole story. Lex had asked her to leave the details to the Pack and she'd agreed. She had serious misgivings at that point in letting the Pack handle it all, but she'd given her word so she kept the details to a minimum.

"No? No enemies? Someone you may have offended back in Ohio?" The detective asked the question with forced casualness but Nina had dealt with enough social workers and cops to know fishing when she saw it. She could also smell something acrid about him.

While Nina felt Lex's arm tense slightly, she knew he'd not appear any different to the man questioning her.

"My crimes were stupid and petty and are over a decade old. I'm sure you also saw that other than juvenile records, I've been clean. Someone I cheated in some street dice game back when I was seventeen is not going to burn down my house and shop.

"Pardon me for doing your job and all," *because you're not* was the unspoken part, "but this is something a hell of a lot bigger than some crap I did a stint in juvie for a decade ago."

"Hey, no need to get defensive. I was just trying to figure out who did this and why. Obviously whoever did this knows you or has some personal issue with you. It's only logical to ask you if you had any information."

"Do you think I would hide information for fun? That it's so enjoyable having my entire life burn down around my ears, threatening my employees? You've done your homework so you know I came from nothing. I worked hard to build my business up, I want to catch who did this more than you do—I promise you that."

Stoner held his hands up in surrender in the face of her anger. "I'll be in touch. I take it you're still staying with Mr. Warden here?" He nodded his chin toward Lex.

"Yes. Ms. Reyes and I are engaged to be married. Our home is her permanent address. You can reach us there day or night. You also have my cell phone number. As you can see, Nina is stressed out and upset. May I take her home or is there anything else you need?"

"Nothing further for now. I'll be in touch." The way he said it made it sound like a threat and Nina sighed.

"Thank you." Nina tiredly leaned into Lex as he led her back to the car. She let him help her inside and put her head back and closed her eyes.

"Beautiful…"

"Don't. Just don't, Lex, because you and I both know this is Carter and if I think about it any more right this moment I'm going to hunt him down and kill him." She said this with her eyes still closed.

"Okay, I know why *I* think it's Carter. Tell me why you do."

"I don't think Melissa is the shooter. She seemed quite genuine with me and while she showed interest in the laptop, her interest didn't seem out of bounds for the situation. She seems happy with being ranked where she is, ambitious but not ruthless."

"Okay." Lex's voice was noncommittal.

"Eric is a tricky one. He pretends to be the man about town with the ladies and yes, he's a bit smarmy. *But*, he listened to every word that was said, even as he checked out my tits."

Lex growled. "Don't think I didn't notice that. Pup. He'll keep away from you in the future if he likes breathing."

Nina opened her eyes and looked at him. "Uh, yeah, whatever. I'd rather have wolves checking my boobs than trying to kill me. Call me shallow that way."

Lex gave a weary sigh and waved her on.

"But Carter, he's a vicious bastard. You can smell the ruthless ambition dripping off him."

"You don't think Melissa is ruthless?" Lex asked, curious.

"Not in the same way that Eric and Carter are. That challenge? Come on! Yes, he was knocked over by a human but so what? He could have turned it around and made himself look benevolent for helping Lex's crazy human mate. But instead he challenges me to the death for it? Overreact much? He wanted to kill me and be done with it. The way he did it was desperate and that's what worries me the most. Because he's at the bottom of the Pack now and he doesn't have the access to the Pack that he used to. Whatever his game is, the people he's working with are so not going to be down with that."

Lex looked in the rearview at his sister. "Meg, what do you think?"

"I think she's right. Carter is hiding something and he's desperate. You can smell it on him. Melissa is comfortable as Fourth now, she isn't hiding anything that is bad enough to stink of it. Eric? He's smart and strong, but too lazy to be behind this.

"The question is—what do we do now as our next step? He's busted down to the lowest echelon of the Pack. He has no ranking at all. We can't watch to see what he's doing with the accounts if he doesn't have the access."

"Desperate people make mistakes. I think it'll be easier to figure him out now that he's going to be taking more risks than before. These Rogues aren't going to just take no for an answer." Lex tapped his finger on the steering wheel as he processed the information.

"Yes. All we have to do is stand back and watch. He'll fuck up and sooner rather than later, I think. The way the money was going in and then out? That's the sign of someone who is living on the margins. That's a dangerous existence. He's bound to get himself out on a limb soon and he'll do something stupid."

Lex glanced at her with a smile. "I love it when you're devious, beautiful."

Nina laughed. "Well, then you're clearly with the right woman."

Instead of continuing east, Lex got off the freeway a few miles early. "Where are we going?"

"I know you're upset and you're tired but I'd like to take you to the range for a bit of practice. Do you know how to use a gun? I mean," he gave her that raised brow before turning back to the road, "I know you can use a shotgun. But do you know how to use a handgun?"

"Uh, well. You do remember me shooting Carter? I believe you were there at the time?" Her voice was sarcastic and he raised a brow. "Yeah. I carried a really old Smith & Wesson back when I was on the streets. It probably wouldn't have shot but it made me feel better. I go to the firing range from time to time but it's not like I'm a big pro or anything."

Lex pulled the car down a long drive. "This is a private range for wolves. We used to use the public one but humans tend to get really nervous when they see us shooting. As a member of the Pack you have access to it and any weapons and ammo you need. The wolf who runs it was one of my mentors when I was growing up."

They parked and Megan got out first. She scanned the area then Lex got out. Nina, growing used to the whole process, waited for Lex to come around to her side.

At the doors to what appeared to be a very nice rambler they stopped and Lex keyed in a series of numbers that Nina surreptitiously watched and noted. Just because she could and it was a hard habit to break.

The door swung open and another, very large man, er, wolf was there, armed to the teeth, er, fangs. He inclined his head. "Enforcer, it's good to have you here."

Lex reached out and touched the man's shoulder. "Grey, it's nice to be here. This is my mate, Nina. She's Rey's sister. She'll be coming in a few times a week to build up her skill level."

The other wolf looked up briefly at Nina. "Welcome to Cascadia. My sincere condolences for your loss. Rey was always fun to play cards with. He watched my youngest last year for a few months on Thursday afternoons when the wife had to work swing shift and I couldn't change my schedule. Taught her how to play backgammon."

A sweet memory rushed through Nina then. Gabriel had loved backgammon. It was one of the games their father had played with them both and it had been a way for Nina and Gabriel to reconnect with him.

She put a hand up to her chest, pressing over her heart. Tears welled up. "Thank you. You don't know what it means to me to hear you say that."

"Ms. Reyes, your brother was a good person. Anyone who said differently didn't know him very well. When I needed him, he always helped out. He may have made a big deal about it or talked a good game, but he refused to take money to watch Bea. Said she kept him young. He would always bring her stuff that he won at the fair or picked up here and there. He told me once that she reminded him of you. Looking at you now, I can see why."

He pulled his wallet out of his back pocket and showed a picture of a smiling little girl with deep brown eyes, wide and filled with a kind of openness that Nina simply couldn't recall ever feeling until that moment. She did have that face for part of her life. For so long it had been too painful to remember and so she just pushed it so far back that she nearly forgot.

"Nina," she whispered and cleared her throat. "Please, call me Nina." She leaned over and hugged the man quickly. "Thank you."

Blushing furiously, he inclined his head again, grinning. Lex rolled his eyes, but seeing Nina's face was worth seeing her hug another man. Pausing mentally, Lex realized that he was one of those people who hadn't known Rey very well. Gabriel Reyes had been a dipshit, but after hearing Nina talk about their past Lex understood Rey a lot better and was sorry he'd never really tried to get to know him.

"Dorian is out back. I'll let him know you're here."

Lex nodded at Grey. "Thanks."

Lex guided Nina through several long hallways until they ended up at a set of large double doors. There was a large locker area to one side and a counter across from that with shelves and shelves of what appeared to be ammunition and firearms. Body armor hung on racks.

"This is the shooting range. There is also an archery range outside for crossbows, very enjoyable. Fencing and sword work is done in a room that we passed on our way in. Hand-to-hand combat work like judo and Krav Maga is done in the smaller practice floors upstairs.

"All of my guards are trained here by Dorian Metz. Dorian has been in charge of training for forty-five years. He's the reason I went into the Army and got into the Rangers. I was hard as nails at nineteen because I'd trained with him my entire life.

"Were we allowed to compete, he is good enough to medal in shooting at the Olympics. He's also a black belt in karate and is incredibly skilled with knives and Japanese long swords.

"I will oversee all your training. But he will help when needed."

Nina wrinkled her nose as Lex began to look over the different handguns behind the counter. "Training?"

Lex chose one and unlocked the trigger lock. He turned and pulled open a drawer, popped out the clip and laid the gun, clip and a box of ammunition down. "You're my mate, Nina. My place in this Pack as Enforcer is a dangerous one. As such, it's dangerous for you too. That means you have to be trained to defend yourself and also to be on the offensive if necessary."

"Okey-dokey. But I hope you know that I'm rebuilding my shop. Not that I don't mind backing you up and kicking anyone's ass who threatens you. But I'm a florist, Lex."

He grinned and kissed her forehead. "I know. But you need to be trained. Everyone in the Pack receives some level of training and everyone ranked Ten and above receives a great deal more."

He then watched her load the bullets into the clip and put the clip into the gun. He had her do it over once more and nodded. "Good."

"Yeah. It's not exactly rocket science."

Just then a man walked through the double doors. "Alexander, my boy! You've brought your mate to me. Are you going to turn her over to my care?"

Nina raised a brow and Lex chuckled. "Dorian!" He hugged the man and turned to Nina. "Dorian Metz, this is Nina, my mate. And *I'll* handle her training. Well, except for swords."

The man was the smallest werewolf Nina had seen. Most of them were at least six feet tall and bulky in some way. Dorian Metz was about five seven. He was totally gray and had the most piercing light blue eyes. He studied her, taking her measure.

"You don't trust me with your stunning little wolf, Alexander?"

Lex snorted. "No, Dorian. My stunning little wolf is tough. She can handle herself quite well. It's you I'm protecting."

Both men laughed and Nina looked at Megan and rolled her eyes.

"Okay, now can you two do the secret handshake already? Or is there spanking involved and some sort of secret ritual?"

Dorian got quiet for a moment and narrowed his eyes at Nina, who actually was beginning to regret her glib comment. Thank goodness his face broke with a huge smile and he pulled her into a hug.

"Oh! I do like this one, Alexander. You need some humor in your life. You've always been too serious. She'll keep you in line, I think."

The rest of their time was spent shooting. Lex was impressed with how well she did. Every shot had hit the target and once he'd begun giving her pointers about how to stand or hold the weapon, she began to improve even more. Clearly she was a natural and her improved reflexes due to the change would help her become an excellent shot.

They'd said their goodbyes and headed back home, where Lex promised a hot bath and Nina heartily endorsed the idea, her muscles already beginning to ache from shooting.

* * * * *

Jack Reed, the Alpha of the Rogue Clan, stared down his nose at Carter. Things had changed in a big way for Jack. Only days before, Carter'd had the upper hand and now not only had the other wolf been busted down to the bottom of the ranks in Cascadia but Warren Pellini, the *spokesperson* from the Pellini Group—read werewolf mob here—came to see him about Carter's debts.

Pellini and Jack had had an interesting discussion about the virus and the cold hard fact that with Carter at the bottom of the Pack, he didn't have access to the records and finances that he had before. That made him more than useless, it made him a liability.

"You did a very stupid thing, Carter."

"Look, how was I to know she'd get a gun and empty an entire clip into me? That bitch needs to get dead and I won't rest until she is." Carter's voice was laced with menace and no small amount of fear.

"The question is, Carter, why the fuck would you think it was a good idea to challenge the Enforcer's mate to the death on the night she was introduced into the Pack?" Jack's hand slammed onto the desk for emphasis.

"It was a great plan! She needs to die, I had the right and the ability to kill her and I took it."

"Yes, a really successful plan, that. Kudos," Jack said dryly.

"So I made a mistake. I'll fix it."

"You can't fix it, Carter. You've lost your position and your power. I can smell their magic on you. They neutered you." Jack's face twisted into a sneer as he referred to the metaphysical stripping of his status and power performed by the governance council.

"I can get it back! You owe me. I got you in. I got you data. I got you the virus when you were just nickel and diming people in two-bit scams. If it weren't for me you wouldn't be sitting on the biggest gold mine ever."

"Yes, yes. And while I appreciate that, your usefulness has come to an end, Carter. You have no further access to the data we need. And we don't need it anymore anyway. The information was key but we can move forward without it. I can offer you a place with the Rogues. We can use runners."

"Runners? How dare you insult me? I'm Third in the largest Pack in the West! I am not a runner!"

Jack reached out and shoved Carter back into the chair. "*Were* Third. And I am aware that you think we're crude and stupid. That we aren't fit to shine your six-hundred-dollar Italian loafers. But the shoe is on the other foot now, pardon the pun. We are smart enough to have engineered the theft and reproduction of the lycanthropy virus. All of those little errands that failed? *You* fucked up. Those failures were caused by your own men and the ones you chose from my ranks. Clearly, Carter, they weren't very well equipped for the job.

"But really, at base? You have no power. You have nothing to offer us. I offer you a place with us because you have nowhere else to go. You can't stay with Cascadia. We both know that you've become a very big liability. I can't just let you stay there. We can't risk exposure."

Jack sat back down and smoothed his tie. "Lastly, you have Lex Warden on your ass. You know as well as I do that he won't rest until you're dead. You tried to kill his mate. I've seen the man rip the fucking head off an opponent without breaking a sweat. Before I left Cascadia I saw a battle. A group of Rogues, my predecessor and his minions actually, launched an attack on Cade and their father. There were nine wolves in full prime and they were armed."

Into the story now, Jack leaned back as he relived the memory of that night eight years before. He took glee in scaring the hell out of Carter with the very real specter of Lex Warden.

"Lex waded into the group and began to change. He began to literally rip the other wolves apart with his bare hands. It was bloody and the screams, my god, I can still hear them today. The Alpha of this Pack challenged Lex and Lex reached out and—I shit you not, Carter—reached out and pulled his motherfucking head right from his body and tossed it down at his feet. Covered with blood, he turned to the remaining wolf who'd fallen to his knees, and grinned. That wolf ran and I never saw or heard of him again.

"Cade and Henri had just watched it all, supremely convinced that Lex would handle the nine wolves. The guard had helped him a bit you understand, but I watched Lex Warden kill six wolves with his bare hands. He never drew a weapon."

Jack stood up and walked around to lean on the corner of his desk. "So you see, you aren't long for this world without the protection of this Pack. Lex Warden is the lycan version of the boogey man and you tried to kill his wife."

"Are you threatening me?" Carter stood, incensed but sweating profusely and shaking after hearing the story he'd heard rumors of for years. "You have no idea who you're dealing with! Who I have behind me. Don't push me, Jack. Don't you dare threaten to kill me. My friends in high places wouldn't like that."

Warren Pellini stepped into the room and nodded once to Jack. He turned his hazel eyes on Carter.

"Warren! Thank god. Did you hear what's happened? These fool Rogues are threatening to kill me! The girl is still alive. That laptop is still out there. If there's anything on it we're fucked." Carter slumped back into the chair and sent a smirk to Jack.

Moments later, it dawned on him. "Warren, what are you doing here? Did you hear of my trouble and come to help? There are ways, you know, for me to get my power back. Spells the old ones can do. Then I can make the last of my payments to you."

Those hazel eyes never flickered with a bit of emotion. In a cool voice Pellini said, "No one is going to perform that spell for you, Carter. Getting your power back would only happen if you performed an extraordinary act for the Pack. And Lex and Cade would be the ones who'd make the final decision. You tried to rip Lex's mate and Cade's anchor apart. Oh, and now she's a wolf. With incredibly high status and power to match, and she's guarded twenty-four hours a day."

Warren leaned against the desk and crossed his ankles with faux casualness. He studied Carter for a few moments. "How far you've fallen, Carter. Sweating in my presence like an unranked wolf. Oh wait, you are an unranked wolf." The laugh that came from his lips was icy.

"Your debt has been discharged. Jack and I have a deal."

Carter stood up. "You've forgiven my debt? Really? Thank..." Carter's eyes blanked and the life fell from them as the silver bullet raced through his brain.

Warren pulled an invisible thread from his suit jacket, looked back at Jack and then nodded to his Enforcer. "Dump it in Cascadia territory. Let it be known that he had a great deal owed due to gambling debt and now that he had no real salary from the Pack he had to pay in another way. That should buy us some time."

"What if they know about the virus?"

Warren shrugged. "If they knew about it, they'd have sent the Enforcer out already, don't you think? The Wardens are nothing if not proactive. I'm betting this laptop is either a fantasy or has nothing on it. Didn't you say there were things built into the program for the lycanthropy virus that would be impossible to break and if they did, just getting in would trigger destruction of the information?"

"For anyone but the finest hackers, yes. The wolf who fed Carter information was a good friend of Tommie's and Tommie told him that the program was unbreakable. The woman is beautiful and strong willed. But she's a florist, she's certainly no hacker." Jack lit a cigar and handed another to Warren.

"You've taken care of the wolves who set that fire at the woman's house and her business?" Warren asked.

"Yes. They won't pose any more of a problem than Carter will. Idiot. Attacking the mate of the Enforcer was a stupid, stupid thing."

"Yes, well. He's no longer an issue for us. The time has come for us to start trials on some humans. We can't very well ransom this virus if it doesn't work."

Chapter Eight

ဢ

Nina slowly sank into the water with a long satisfied sigh. The water was just hot enough. Her core body temperature was starting to rise as Lex had explained it would. That part was kind of nice as she was one of those people who was always cold.

She'd just closed her eyes and fully relaxed her body when she heard Lex enter their bedroom and kick the door closed. The new intensity of her senses was a bit overwhelming and she wondered what it would be like once she fully made the change.

He entered the bathroom and her body tightened up and her insides calmed as his scent hit her. It was like he was this cherished thing and the hottest, sexiest man to ever walk the planet—warm milk and Brad Pitt all in one.

"What are you smiling about?" he asked softly.

"Warm milk," she answered opening her eyes to see him there with a mug and a plate with cookies on it. She certainly wasn't going to say Brad Pitt. Lex came bearing chocolate chip cookies and chai tea, milky and sweet like she preferred it. Hell, he was better than Brad Pitt.

"Do you want some warm milk?" He started to move back toward the door and she put her hand up.

"No. Thank you, darlin', but no. I was just thinking that you were like a hot sex symbol and comforting warm milk all at the same time."

The worry passed from his face and those lips quirked up a grin. "You looking to get lucky, ma'am? You're looking pretty damned good there naked and wet."

"Oh, now, you see, I think I'm already getting lucky here with this plate of cookies in the hands of an incredibly sexy man."

"You're full of shit. But I like it. Cade made them, he bakes when he's upset."

Nina opened her mouth to say something but closed it and slid beneath the water. When she came back up Lex was staring at her with a raised eyebrow and a smirk.

"You were going to say?"

"You know what I was going to say, therefore it isn't nearly as fun." She grabbed a cookie and stuffed it into her mouth. "And anyway, his girly ways make good chocolate chip cookies so who am I to complain that he's the amazing baking Alpha?"

Lex chuckled and started to head out.

"Uh, hello?"

He turned around. "What is it, beautiful?"

"Is the honeymoon over so fast? Before we've even had a wedding?"

He looked confused.

She sighed. "Lex, it's midafternoon and a naked woman is in your bathtub. You were planning to...? Grout? Go bake? Shine your obscenely expensive shoes? Ravish your wife?"

She got to her knees and held out her hand. "I think you're dirty. Really dirty. You need a bath."

"Oh! Well you were tired and you had a crappy morning and..."

"Babbling again."

Laughing, he tossed his clothes off and got into the deep tub with her with a wince. "Damn it, Nina, this water is hot."

Rolling her eyes, she moved over and straddled his lap. "Thank you for the cookies." She kissed one eyelid. "And the tea." She kissed the other. "Thank you for being concerned about me." His lips were beneath hers and felt carnal and fleshy and delicious. She grazed them with her teeth and he opened his mouth and pulled her to his chest tightly.

"You taste so good, beautiful," he murmured against her lips and then her chin and neck as she tipped her head back, allowing him access to the hollow of her throat. As she did it, she felt her wolf move within her. Be *moved* within her by the submissive act of baring her neck to him.

He growled low, the sound trickling from his lips. With gentle but firm teeth, he took the tendon at the side of her neck and bit down. A shudder of orgasmic pleasure rolled through her, she whimpered as the sensuality of the moment flooded her.

"Oh, Nina, god." Lex moaned, leaning his forehead against her breastbone, panting.

"What? Lex, fuck me now. No foreplay, no preamble. Hard, deep and fast. I need you to." She stood and he looked up her body into her face. His pupils were wide and his normally green eyes were deeper, the flecks of gold more pronounced.

"Nina, my wolf is very close to the surface. It's near the full moon and with the claiming and your change, it... I don't know if I can be gentle right now. Just let me catch my breath."

She reached down and grabbed his cock in her hand, her face nose to nose with his. "Did I say I wanted gentle?"

He stood so quickly she didn't even see it. She found herself facing the wall, slightly bent, hands flat against the tile above her head. He leaned over her and kissed the back of her neck while his fingers tested her readiness. His breath quickened to find her so wet and as she'd asked, the head of his cock found her gate and nudged into her body.

Hips tilting, her body gave invitation and she was unable to stop another whimper of entreaty as he braced his hands at her hips and took her the rest of the way in one long thrust.

Hard and fast, he fucked into her body, hilting with each long thrust. The excitement at being so used by him—no, not used—possessed, wanted, desired by him, was overwhelming.

Moving one of his hands, he placed it, palm cupping her pubic bone so that his fingers slipped over her clit with each dig into her body. This brought a violent shudder of sensation with each pass.

"Is this what you wanted, Nina?" he said low into her ear.

"Yes," she hissed as the first sensations of her orgasm began to manifest. "You feel so good, Lex. Please, more."

"More?" he asked, lips at her ear. "More what?"

"Fuck me. Harder. I need you to be in me harder."

And he bit her again, this time across the back of her neck, essentially holding her in place as he fucked her. Climax rocketed through her system. Her eyes closed against it as the tide pulled her under. She wondered what that scream was until she realized it was her own. Her cells swelled with endorphins, pussy slick with honey to ease his way, inner walls clasping and fluttering around his invading cock.

"Jesus, Nina, that's so good," he growled around her neck and thrust one last time as he unleashed his own orgasm deep into her body.

For several long minutes afterward, they stood there, still entwined in each other, regaining breath. When Lex pulled out he was gentle.

Bending down, he opened the drain as he turned on the shower head. "Let me get your hair."

He washed her hair as she leaned against him. Afterward, he helped her out, handing her a warm, fluffy towel. There was a sore spot on her neck and she turned, catching sight of the bruise where he'd bitten her.

"Oh..." she said quietly, touching it.

He paled. "Oh, Nina, I'm sorry. I didn't tell you beforehand. It's…the biting…it happens when your wolf is close mpf…"

She put her fingers over his lips. "You didn't hurt me. I liked it. It's okay. I understand. I understood while you were doing it."

He took her hand and kissed it. "Oh. Good. Because I liked doing it. We heal quickly but there's some arnica in here for bruises." He dug in the medicine cabinet and pulled out a tube.

"Do you often bruise women while fucking them in your bathroom?" she asked, surprised by the edge in her voice.

He turned quickly and she felt that tug low in her gut that she'd grown to realize was her wolf and his reacting to each other. "Beautiful, you may have noticed that my life is sort of dangerous? I have the arnica for my own bruises." He took her chin in his palm and kissed her lips.

"There were others before you, yes. But there was no one until you. Do you understand what I'm saying?"

She shook her head.

"Nina, before you I never spent the night with women. I had sex and left. I didn't bring them here. They served a purpose and it was a body-to-body thing. You are everything. Body, soul, heart to my body, soul and heart. You're it. *We're* it."

"Wow." She blinked back tears. "You say the best stuff."

He chuckled and dabbed on the arnica cream.

* * * * *

Back in their bedroom, Nina stood at the dresser and looked back over her shoulder at him. "You know," she said, dropping her robe, "aside from the insurance adjuster coming out later on, I'm free for the next few hours."

Lex hummed in agreement as he walked toward her, dropping the towel that had been wrapped around his waist. He picked her up and took her to the bed, laying her down, following her so that his body was resting on hers.

"How is it that I want you less than ten minutes after I've had you?" he murmured, delivering small kisses to her lips.

"I don't know but I'm going to stock up on that soap so you keep it up. Heh, you know what I mean."

He laughed then and rolled so that she was on top.

She'd just dipped to steal another kiss when Cade yelled up the stairs for Lex. It sounded urgent enough that she didn't complain, just rolled off and stayed out of his way as he pulled on jeans and a T-shirt and left the room.

She quickly pulled on some clothes, pulled her wet hair back and followed the voices into the office where Cade, Lex and several other Pack wolves had gathered and were having a terse discussion.

Lex looked up when she walked in. "Carter's body was just found near my parents' place in North Bend."

Nina raised an eyebrow and went to pour herself a cup of coffee. She opened her mouth and then shut it again quickly. What could she say? Good? She certainly wasn't sorry, but at the same time, she knew enough to know it couldn't bode well for the Pack.

She sat on the arm of the chair Cade was in and, changing her mind, put the mug in front of him and got up to get herself another. She shot a look at Lex and held up the pot but he shook his head.

Settling back in, she realized that the warmth and appreciation she'd felt was from Cade and that she was supposed to still be pissed at him. She gave a mental shrug. She'd punish him later for fun. Now was the time for unity.

"This is clearly a message, Alpha. I know there's something going on and we can't deal with it effectively if we don't know what is happening," one of the other wolves—Eric? Derek?—said to Cade.

"Message?"

Lex turned to Nina. "He was shot in the back of the head with silver shot and left openly in Pack territory. That's a not-so-good sign that the mafia is involved."

"The mafia? What would organized crime care about werewolves and coffee?"

"The werewolf mafia." Lex turned to Cade as Nina processed that one.

The werewolf mafia? They had to be kidding! It was so absurd she fought the urge to laugh.

"None of these wolves were Carter's. We need to tell them. Derek is right. This has gone too far. The more secrets we keep, the worse it's going to be."

Cade sighed and nodded. Lex explained the missing virus, the laptop and the embezzlement, and the other wolves sat down in shock.

"And obviously at this point we know Carter had something to do with it. I mean, you don't get tapped by the mob, furry or not, if you're a nice wolfie boy from Seattle just minding your own business." Nina thought it over.

"Yes. The real question is at this point, what's next for the Rogues?" Lex paced the room as he spoke.

"Well, if I were them, I'd want to make sure the virus was ready. Was it?"

"We obviously hadn't done human trials yet. We were trying to set something up with humans who had been infected involuntarily. It doesn't happen all that often and there are ethics that need to be minded."

Except for her brother. She wanted to remind them that Gabriel hadn't been asked to be changed but she let it go. She nodded. "Okay. And what about the effect on wolves?"

Lex winced. "That would be some creepy shit, Nina, if we'd given it to wolves not knowing what would happen."

"Duh. I didn't ask if you'd gone all creepy evil scientist. I just didn't know if you'd had any extrapolations by your scientists about what may happen."

The other wolves in the room stiffened when Nina popped off to Lex. Lex brooked no disrespect and they hadn't ever seen anyone other than Cade speak to him like that before. In fact, most of them acted utterly terrified of him, which made her laugh, but she'd seen enough of him to know that how he treated her and those who he was close to was very different than how he treated enemies.

Nina noticed and laughed. "Don't worry, I still think he's the big bad wolf. I'm just snotty, I can't help it."

"And you're Second, too," Cade said with a shrug and a grin.

"Oh yeah, I am."

Lex groaned. "Can we not give her any ammo right now and keep focused on the problem at hand?"

Nina snickered and nodded. "Of course, darling."

He snorted and began to pace again.

"Back to the subject," he shot a raised eyebrow at Nina, "the researchers were divided. Some of them felt it would be harmless because it was already in our systems, the others felt it would be like a viral agent, causing our systems to turn on themselves. Obviously we couldn't test that and endanger wolves any more than we wanted to endanger humans."

"Jesus, we've just handed a potential tool of bioterrorism to the Rogues," Dave said.

"Worse, to the mob." Lex pushed a hand through his hair and Nina's insides tightened at the sight. Damn man was like a drug.

"Well, what we have to do is clear. We have to get it back. How we're going to do it is another thing." Nina stood and stretched her hands above her head.

"*We* aren't going to do anything," Lex growled.

Nina looked at him and then to Cade. "Listen, I have skills here. I'm not some helpless bimbo."

"I'm not saying you're helpless. I'm saying you aren't going to get involved in crossfire between us, the mob and these Rogues. They're brutal, Nina. Snotty or not, I happen to like you in one piece," Lex said with strained calm.

"May I speak with you outside, please?" Nina asked, sugary sweet.

Lex looked at her and knew she'd say whatever it was on her mind in front of everyone if he didn't go with her, so he sighed. "I'll be back in a few minutes," he told Cade and waved toward the door where Nina preceded him.

Nina was waiting in their bedroom, arms crossed, tapping a foot. "Shut the door."

He narrowed his eyes and did it. "I'm not going to argue with you about this, Nina. I'm the Enforcer for this Pack and I say who is involved in anything like this."

"Oh I couldn't possibly care less, Lex. I'm going to be involved whether you like it or not. Now, we can do this the easy way or the hard way. It's all the same to me. My brother was killed over this. I was almost killed and now I'm a werewolf because of Carter and your stupid fucking werewolf rules. I will have my day here and if you think you can pull rank and swing your dick around and play the big macho wolf to shut me up, you're out of your mind."

"You think you can tell me how to do my job?" he growled through clenched teeth.

She rolled her eyes but took a deep breath for calm. "Alexander Warden, I am not telling you how to do your job. Believe it or not, I respect your job very much. I respect that you do it so well that people fall over themselves in fear and reverence every time you enter a room. But, babe, I am telling you that I have skills here that can help. Have your people gone to Carter's and taken his computer? Have you taken his computer from his workspace? I can get in and see what he's been up to. I can help. Please, let me help."

How is it that she always knew just how to disarm him? He was touched and flattered and utterly frustrated by this woman. "Why are you so damned difficult? I just want to keep you safe!" he thundered.

"Look, Mister Shouty, don't get all testosterone wild on me! I didn't say I would go in guns a blazin'. But you need to separate your feelings for me as your mate and your understanding that I have the ability to help you here. If you wanted some sweet, easygoing woman you barked up the wrong tree. Heh, barked! Anyway, suck it up, you have me and I'm not sweet but if you play your cards right, I am easy."

That pulled a smile from him and he sighed deeply. "Okay, so if I get you the computer stuff you'll let me do the other stuff without interfering?"

"By stuff you mean what?"

"God, you should have been a lawyer. I mean, I handle the physical stuff. I plan whatever plan to storm the Rogues or the mafia and you stay here or wherever I say, safe."

"For now, I agree. Since I no longer have a store to run, I have the time to crack some computers."

"Why do I have the feeling I've just given you the keys to the castle?"

She got a sour look. "Keys to the castle? Dude, work on your metaphors." She crossed the room and walked out and down the stairs toward the office where the other wolves were and Lex couldn't help but admire her, even as she took ten years off his life with her antics.

* * * * *

181

True to his word, Lex had Carter's laptop and home computer brought to the house for Nina to examine. His books and work computer were also delivered. An office was set up for her in the room that had served as the guestroom when she first came to the house.

Lex put Megan on Nina permanently so he could investigate the situation without worry. He extracted a promise from Nina that she wouldn't leave the grounds without his knowledge.

Tracy stayed over at the house and helped out with some of the records investigation and other tasks that Nina set her on. Both Lex and Cade were impressed by their baby sister's competence and intelligence. They saw her through new eyes as she worked with Nina.

As the full moon approached, Nina's restlessness increased. She found that she needed to be outside more often, even if it was just to walk on the decks outside the main rooms of the house.

She was afraid to admit to herself just how terrified she was of the first transformation. She'd endured a lot in her life but this change into something totally different freaked her out more than she could wrap her head around. She didn't want to make Lex feel any guiltier than he already did. She was angry, yes, but she'd come to her own peace over the way she'd been transformed. It was that or hate Lex and what she'd become, and that way was the destruction of her entire future. No, she had to accept it, it was done. But it still freaked her right out.

The work was fairly easy for Nina. Carter thought he was clever but he wasn't really. His passwords were stupid and easily gotten around. The firewall and other security he had was not very complicated.

The day before the full moon Nina headed into Lex's office, dropped a sheaf of papers on his desk and flopped into a chair until he finished his phone call.

Lex turned to her and smiled. She was so damned beautiful that he still marveled at the sight of her. His once prim schoolmarm was a goddess and he caught fire in her presence.

"Good afternoon, beautiful."

She rolled her eyes at his flattery and smiled as it won her over despite herself. "Flatterer."

He laughed. "Does it get me laid?"

She snorted. "I bet it always did before me, too. Now, to business you pervert." She leaned over his desk and pointed at a column of numbers. "Your boy had quite a problem in Vegas. The left-hand column there is what he lost, the right-hand column is what he owed and that far tally is what was coming in. From what I can tell, those numbers from the Swiss accounts were payments he received and from what I can tell, he gambled them away."

"Okay. Tell me how you know it was gambling."

She shuffled through the papers until she found what she was looking for and put it in front of him. "He kept pretty good records, actually. The dates he stayed in Vegas at these three hotels coincide with the huge amounts of money debiting his accounts. I took the liberty of, uh, nosing around a bit in some databases and verified the times he was there and the payouts when he did win. They have to keep records of that sort of thing you know, for the IRS."

"How did you...never mind, I don't want to know. Okay. So we have a situation where he was in need of money. How did he jump from that to involvement with the Rogues and the mob?"

"Well, I don't know the hows and whys of it. What I did find were notations of deposits from a J. R. and a W. P. The numbers got bigger and bigger, Lex. Carter was in deep. From what I could find, he was in the process of losing his home. He was so far behind on his car payments he was going to get it repossessed."

"He made quite a handsome salary. And, wait, did he have all of this financial stuff in his computer?"

Nina looked at him and sighed, waving his question away. "I saw what you paid him. He went through that in the first ten days of every month. When he wasn't in Vegas—and he used your private jet to fly out, by the way—he played video poker and used some of the tribal casinos around here. He hadn't made a payment on his mortgage in five months."

Nina pulled out another sheet of paper. "Here is where your Pack funds began to siphon off. It was small amounts at first, but just before you pulled his access he stole seventeen grand. All in all, it appears that he embezzled roughly forty thousand dollars from the Pack coffers."

Lex sat back in disbelief. "My god, Nina. I can't believe he'd do this. You don't have any idea how strong the compulsion to serve the Pack is when you're this high up."

"Oh I don't? Because I'm not a wolf?" Hurt arced through her at his blasé dismissal of what she was dealing with.

"You're right, I'm sorry. So you do see. I don't get it."

"Come on, Lex. You have Rogues, they appear to live in the same basic configuration that you all do, with an Alpha and upper ranks. If they're so bad, they must have resisted the compulsion. Your problem is that you don't think like you're bent. That's why you're lucky to have me, because I do."

She pulled out another sheet. "Now, these are the records from your labs and it appears that three vials of the virus are missing. The lead researcher there claims he reported that a month ago. This after he'd reported some tampering with their internal records two months back."

"Reported it to Carter?"

"Yep. But Lex, this system is just flimsy. You're dealing with what are essentially biowarfare agents here, and I could get in and look around with no problem at all. They gave me all this information over the phone without any real verification of who I was. That's why you're in the situation you are now."

"You're totally wasted as a florist." The admiration in his voice salved the hurt feelings she'd had.

"I am a damned good florist. By the way, the plants you have at the Pack house are crap. But you know, I can't be sniffing around computers very often, at least not the internet. It's not good for me to expose myself like that."

Alarmed, he stood up and shot around the desk. "Why are you risking yourself! Nina, stop it now."

"Lex, it's okay. Most of the stuff I'm doing is all internal. I'm a good investigator, you know. I can spot a scam miles away and I can talk my way around most anyone. Including grumpy, overprotective werewolves." She gave him a quick kiss. "But thank you for your concern, it's very sweet."

"Sweet? Jesus, Nina, are you trying to push me over the edge? Be careful! Let someone else do the work if it'll get you in trouble. And for god's sake, don't expose the Pack with all of this. The last thing I need are the human cops breathing down my neck."

"Is that how little you think of me? That this is a lark for me? All fun and games and I don't care a thing about you or your precious Pack?" She stood and headed for the door but he blocked her way.

"You are not going to run from me again. Why do you take everything the wrong way?"

"Excuse me? Why do *I* take everything the wrong way? Why do *you* assume I'd do anything to expose your family? I nearly died for your precious family, Lex. I am being very careful but you need this information."

Leaning down to put his forehead against hers, he exhaled slowly. "You are my family, Nina. You're part of us and I didn't assume that you'd expose us. It was just something I said. I tell my men to be careful all the time, it's part of my job. I didn't mean to imply that you would endanger us."

The tension went out of her then at his words and her arms wrapped around him.

"Are you ready for the transformation tomorrow?" he murmured into her ear.

"I have no idea, Lex. Truthfully, I'm scared to death."

He led her back to the couch and sat down, pulling her into his lap. "Beautiful, there's nothing to be scared of. Your wolf is already there, you can feel it. You'll just sort of let her take over for a while. You won't do anything you don't want to do. It's not like you'll be a different person."

"Lex, I'm going to be a werewolf. No offense, but that in and of itself is something I don't want to do. And if turning into a fucking wolf from a human isn't becoming a different person, I don't know what is."

He looked puzzled, then annoyed and finally resigned. "Okay, all of those things are accurate to a certain extent. But the fact is that you are already a werewolf and what I meant was that your values and your mind and heart won't change when you're in wolf form."

"If you say so."

"I do. And you'll see tomorrow night." He kissed the top of her head. "For now, I need to make some discreet calls. I think Jack Reed and Warren Pellini are the J. R. and W. P. noted in Carter's files. Jack is the Alpha of the Rogues and Warren is the Second in the mob."

She stood up, throwing her hands in the air. "This situation gets more jacked up every minute." Nina left the room grumbling to herself about werewolf godfathers and Rogues.

Chapter Nine

ॐ

Nina's eyes fluttered open to focus on Lex's face right above her own, looking intently down at her.

She smiled. "Hey."

He leaned down and kissed her. It was slow at first, drawing her into his web. He wooed her lips with his own. He tasted her, sipped her with the barest of pressure. Her eyelids slowly closed as she let him take her wherever he was going.

Her hands slid up the warm, hard line of his torso, up the rippled muscle of his back. He was hers, she felt that particularly strongly at that moment. In fact, despite her extreme discomfort at moments over her predicament and her feelings about the way she was changed, she hadn't doubted him or what they were to each other for some time. That surety was calming, comforting, it anchored her in much the way Cade did. Gave her security.

When the hot wet of his tongue scalded her lips she opened her mouth to his, opening herself to him, giving herself to him. His taste shot through her system, filling her senses, intoxicating her.

The sensual slide of flesh on flesh as she arched beneath him, as her tongue slid along his, of his hair through her fingers — delighted her.

The kiss deepened, the pressure of his lips became firmer, more insistent as the edge of his teeth caught her lip. She was swept away by the intensity of his passion and could do little more than cling to him as he devoured her.

Her skin tingled and her bones ached so that she arched hard with it, a surprised cry coming from deep within her stomach.

He pulled back from the kiss and looked down at her. Staring up into his eyes, she fell into his gaze. There she saw his wolf and knew that the feelings she'd just experienced was her own wolf clawing to the surface.

She sighed with that knowledge, with the feeling of her wolf rolling within her skin, reaching out to Lex's. A low growl trickled from his lips and she blinked up into his face. There was no fear, only recognition of that more feral nature, of what was now the other half of her being, and it matched his—this man who loomed over her so strong and intense. Yet she felt no threat from him.

"Lex," she murmured and blinked slowly as her body adjusted to the dual-natured feeling, of forest and loam, of city and sidewalk, of two legs and four, of flesh and fur. It was like looking through the bottom of a very thick glass and seeing things in multiples.

"Beautiful, can you feel it?" His teeth were white and sharp against the olive of his complexion. He was so incredibly handsome at that moment, so compelling to her, the lure of his sexuality, of his very being tugged at her. It almost felt as if it was happing to someone else and she was watching it on screen as she reached out and slid her palm around his neck, pulling him down to her.

"Yes, I can feel it. I can feel her inside of me."

"Are you scared?" This was whispered, his lips the barest distance from hers.

"No. I want you, Lex. Make me yours."

"You already are, Nina. Before you even laid eyes on me." His words halted as his lips were on hers again and his hands were alive over her body. He touched her with wonder, with reverence and awe and she pressed into him, not able to get enough of him, wanting him so much she was sure she'd die of it.

His lips moved to the sensitive spot below her ear and she arched back, baring her neck to him, understanding the relevance of that act more now than ever. He bit the tendon there where neck meets shoulder and she shuddered as pleasure roiled through her body.

Her nails dug into the hard muscle at his shoulders as wordless sounds of pleasure slid from her mouth.

His tongue blazed a scalding trail down the hollow of her throat to find a nipple. He flicked it with the tip over and over until she was begging him for more, begging him to take her, to make love to her, to possess her as deeply as he could.

He responded, sucking the nipple deep into his mouth, teeth grazing it. One of his hands slid down her stomach and over the flesh of her mound and between her thighs. They both gasped when his fingertips found her pussy, hot and wet and ready for him. Two fingers thrust into her and his thumb found her clit, swollen and hard, slippery and sensitive.

The walls of her pussy clutched at his fingers as she hooked her calf around his ass, opening herself up to his touch.

"More. Please, Lex. More," she gasped out.

"Okay, beautiful." He moved down then, tongue licking over the flesh of her stomach, over that very sensitive crease where thigh met body.

When he pulled his hand away she cried out at his absence only to moan in pleasure as his mouth closed over her.

The intensity of that feeling—of the wet of his mouth meeting the wet of her pussy, of the sinuous slide of his tongue as it slid through the folds of her body that way, tasting her like she was the best thing on earth—made her entire body tremble.

She could feel the scalding heat of her own honey as he drew a thumb through it and slid it down to the sensitive flesh of her rear passage. She stiffened and he looked up at her.

"I mean to have all of you. You told me to make you mine, Nina. You are mine. Your pleasure is my job. Give yourself to me, beautiful. Trust me."

She nodded and her head fell back as he took a long lick, the flat of his tongue applying hard pressure over her clit. The spark of orgasm began to heat her body, seep into her.

While he suckled her clit, teasing the underside with the tip of his tongue, his thumb pressed into her ass. He stroked it gently into her until she began to relax and accept the new sensations he delivered.

His teeth abraded her clit gently but firmly and orgasm slammed through her, poured into her cells until they all exploded as endorphins surged through her body. Stars burst onto her eyelids as her skin tingled and heated. Her bones, once achy, now felt nearly fluid as her back arched, and she couldn't help but scream out his name.

She was still lost in the swirl of pleasure when he moved up and entered her, his cock sliding into her body, her flesh parting like a molten curtain around his.

"Damn, you're so hot. So tight and wet. You feel so good I may die from it," he murmured as he bent and licked the sweat from her collarbone.

Her body slid beneath his, the sweat of their exertion easing the friction. She was past words by that point. The wolf inside her was pushing her to submit to him and she couldn't argue. All she wanted was for him to make love to her. All she craved was the weight of his body on her own, the slide of his cock deep within her. The scent of his heated flesh rode her in much the same way he did. She was utterly drowning in sensation. Drowning in Lex.

His pupils were so large they made his eyes look black. His wolf was there, just inside him, and for a brief moment she felt her own wolf rush up and stroke against his and they both gasped and then moaned at the pleasure.

Over and over his cock slid deep within her body. There were no coherent words, just her moans and sobs for more and his growls and gasps. The wet collision of bodies was the only other sound in the room.

It felt like being pulled into a vortex, the only thing holding her in place, keeping her from being swept away entirely, was the way his cock pinned her to this reality. Her heart beat with his, her lungs breathed with his, their scents mingled and became one.

It built and built, the tension tightened, the web of desire, of lust and love and longing—of *belonging*—built until it burst over them both as he shouted her name, his body emptying into hers in pulse after pulse.

A feedback loop of sensation was created and orgasm spread over them both in wave after wave over what seemed like minutes until he collapsed with a long sigh just next to her, chest heaving, cock still buried within her.

* * * * *

Some point later she awoke again and sighed with satisfaction. His head was on her chest, ear over her heart. The sight made her ache with tenderness for him. She couldn't remember the last time she'd felt tenderness and tears began to come then.

He looked up with a start, worry on his face. "Nina? Honey? Did I hurt you?"

She shook her head, reaching out to trace a fingertip over his lips. "No. Just the opposite. You healed me. I've never, ever, felt that way before. Thank you."

If Lex Warden hadn't already adored the prickly woman in his arms, he would have fallen right then at the expression of her feelings in such an open way. She'd been so closed up that he didn't know what to do with the rush of awe and admiration he felt for her.

"Nina, I've never felt that way before either. That was... I don't even have the words to describe what it felt like to make love to you just now. The way our wolves touched and reacted... I love you, beautiful."

More tears came then. Resigned, Lex accepted it because women always seemed to do the opposite of what he expected. They cried at the oddest moments, but he knew these tears were a gift from her heart. That she trusted him with her barest emotions.

"It wasn't like this for you with all the wolves that you've been with?"

"No. Even so close to a full moon, my wolf has never surfaced like that. When I awoke and saw you there I just wanted to look at you for hours. When I was inside you, when I was tasting you—it was everything. It was all I ever wanted. You fulfill me in a way I never even knew I needed."

She smiled up at him and had reached to pull him back to her when his phone began to ring.

She groaned and he growled but moved to pick it up anyway. He still had a job to do but if it wasn't life or death, he'd kill whoever it was calling him.

Nina watched him and heard the caller on the other end. She got up and quickly headed into the shower and was moving out of the way by the time he walked in.

"You heard?" His face was grim as he stood under the spray and she toweled off quickly.

"Yes. Lex, what does this mean?"

"I don't know but I'm afraid it doesn't bode well for us. Stoner is involved now and we'll have to talk to him about the situation. He's going to meet me at the hospital in an hour."

"Okay, I'll get dressed and meet you downstairs."

"Nina, it's too close to the full moon. Stay here." He stepped out of the shower and clenched his teeth when he saw that she'd already left the room.

She was downstairs waiting near the doors to the garage when he came down some short minutes later.

"Nina, it's too close…"

"Don't waste your breath, Scooby. I'm coming. I already spoke to Cade, he said I won't be in danger of changing until at least eight tonight. As it's just now nine in the morning, I'm just fine."

Lex spun and saw his brother leaning against the doorway to the living room.

"What? She asked! I didn't know she was trying to make some end run around you until she said, 'HA!' and stomped in here to wait for you."

"Don't look so pleased, Cade. You are so going to get yours when your mate comes around."

"Shut up and be thankful. Now go on and give me a full report when you get it."

Lex inclined his head for a moment and looked to Nina. "You see, I told him he needs to stay here and he does. He's an alpha. You don't have that excuse and you don't listen worth a damn."

Nina rolled her eyes. "Are you done Professor Mc Lecture? Because time's a wastin' while you're going all stern on me." She turned and walked out. Lex sent a one fingered salute to his brother over his shoulder as he followed in her wake.

He gave the signal to two of his men to keep an eye on the house, and Megan hopped into the backseat to ride to the hospital with them.

* * * * *

Once they parked, Lex did a quick visual sweep and opened the door, holding down the locks on Nina's side until he'd taken a quick but deep scent of the air around the car. No other wolves had been there and other than the cops, there was no scent of gun oil, metal from weapons or gunpowder. He nodded at Megan and released the locks and Nina got out.

She walked to his side and he was relieved to see how aware she was of her surroundings and how close she stayed to him. Far enough from his right arm for him to be able to draw quickly but close enough to him to push her wherever he needed to if he had to keep her safe.

"I'll do the talking."

"Okay. I'll just stand in the background and look pretty, shall I?" She arched a brow at him.

"Must you always be so argumentative?"

"Must you be a furry fascist? Jeez! Look, furbutt, I am not a moron. I've been tap dancing around cops for a very long time, thank you very much. Now shut up and pull that stick out of your ass, why don't you?"

Megan studiously looked at the entrance doors.

"You know, you seriously try my patience. When you talk to me like that in front of my men, it's bad for morale."

"Lex, she's your sister. She knows you're a control freak. I bet you were a control freak at six years old, too. But she'd take a bullet for you in a heartbeat. That's morale. Now, shall we continue to argue or go in and talk to Stoner?" She did make a mental note to cut back on being sassy to him in front of the non-family members of the Pack, though. He was right that it would be bad for morale if she did it.

He heaved a sigh and growled his assent. She grinned in triumph and he shook his head as they walked inside together.

The special unit for humans infected by the lycanthropy virus was on the top floor of the hospital and had special secured entrances. Lex was familiar with the unit as he was the Pack's liaison to the human authorities if and when a human was infected, whether intentionally or not.

He turned to explain it to Nina and saw the tightness of her lips. "Do you want to wait outside? Nothing is going to hurt you in here, the security is really first-rate and I'm with you."

"I know what it's like in here."

It struck him then that she'd been there when Gabriel had been infected some years before by a member of Cascadia Pack. He wondered for a brief moment why he hadn't seen her, but if she'd been wearing that schoolmarm disguise and he'd been there on Pack business, he probably looked right past her.

He squeezed her hand and kissed her fingertips and she gave him a small smile.

They saw Detective Stoner standing in the hallway near the nurses' station. He looked tired.

"Mr. Warden. Ms. Reyes." He nodded at them and then at Megan. He held out a hand to point them down the hall. "He's in a room down here. One of your doctors is with him now with a human doctor."

Lex gave a short nod and they walked down the quiet hallway to the last room on the right and entered.

The memories of Gabriel's near-death experience there flooded Nina and her heart squeezed in her chest as she saw the man in the bed. But this man had no visible bandages. His face was slightly bruised but it was fading.

Dr. Molinari looked up and inclined her head to them both in much the same way Lex had done to Cade earlier.

She shook her head and they all walked into the room next door and closed it behind them.

"The man has no external scratches or bites. He has two needle marks on his inner arm. He tests positive for the lycanthropy virus." The other doctor, Nina assumed the human doctor, told them.

Lex looked to Dr. Molinari, who nodded surreptitiously.

"You want to tell me how this could be?" Detective Stoner asked. "I thought the victim had to be bitten. That there was something in the saliva and the adrenaline that created the right environment for the virus to take hold. We've been told that humans, even if stuck with a needle that had been in a werewolf or had werewolf blood on it, wouldn't change. Are you telling me they lied to us? That *you* lied to us?"

Lex sighed. "No. Not exactly. If you went into that room and the doctor took blood from him and injected it straight into you, you wouldn't be infected. The virus has to have the right circumstances to grow and infect the DNA of a human host.

"But late last year our scientists were able to manipulate the virus. This was to create a vaccine or antibody so that if a human was infected without his or her permission they could receive the treatment and halt the transformation.

"In order to do this, they created a live virus that could, if injected directly, infect the host without a bite or saliva or adrenaline. Up until now, it was theoretical that it would work."

"Are you telling me that this man was experimented on? Does the human government know about this?" Stoner thundered.

Lex's eyes flashed angrily. "No! We would not do such a thing. Has he been questioned? What happened?"

"He's been dosed with a very heavy narcotic. He appears to have been a street person. He hasn't regained consciousness for very long. There are issues of malnourishment and some exposure-related problems. He was quite bruised up when we found him late last night. He said wolves got him, which is why we brought him here and tested him. But the bruises have been healing and we can't find any trauma sites that are consistent with an attack. I suppose now we know why. I'm guessing that the reasons the needle marks haven't healed as quick as the other trauma stems from the interaction of the virus," the human doctor stated.

"Tonight is the full moon. Someone from the Pack will be here to help him but he'll need to stay here for another few days," Dr. Molinari assured Stoner.

"I thought you did that?" Stoner looked to Lex.

"Normally I would. Two of my men will be here in my stead with our Third. Tonight is also the first time Nina will change. As her mate, I will be with her."

Stoner looked quickly at Nina and then covered his surprise. "I didn't know you were a werewolf, too, Ms. Reyes."

"It's a recent thing, Detective Stoner." Nina didn't elaborate further. What could she tell him without getting the Pack into trouble?

He gave her a long look that she knew was taking her measure, putting things together and trying to work out just what was happening. She also felt, instinctively, that Detective Ben Stoner was a man that could be trusted to do the right thing. And Nina truly believed that the Pack needed to talk straight with Stoner regarding the whole virus thing. But she wasn't on her own anymore and she didn't have the right to say anything until she'd spoken to Lex.

It should have chafed more, she'd been on her own for a very long time. Instead, it felt okay, comfortable even, that she had other people to consider. It wasn't the weight of dependency like it had been with Gabriel. Rather, the cooperative nature of the Pack. She felt a part of it instead of responsible for it. It dawned on her then, that she was accepting both her wolf and the fact that she was a part of the Pack. It still hurt, but it was something she was making room in her life for.

Lex watched her out of the corner of his eye. He could tell she wanted to elaborate and steeled himself, but she stayed quiet after answering Stoner's question very simply. Will wonders never cease? He stifled a smile at her nature and focused on the conversation again.

"So, you have any idea how this virus ended up in the guy in the next room?"

Lex had debated this with Cade earlier and with himself over and over. The way this information was dealt with was crucial to them as a Pack and also to interspecies relations with the humans for years to come. Some things couldn't be hidden and now that a human had been involved he was going to have to take a leap of faith.

Nina squeezed his arm and nodded ever-so slightly and he exhaled. "Can you come out to the house, Detective? There are some things we'd like to show you."

Stoner looked at him carefully for several long moments and finally nodded. "Let's go. I can't wait to hear this one."

Lex nodded and looked toward Dr. Molinari. "I'm going to order two men be stationed here and I'll send Eric over immediately. We'll usher him in and offer him a place in the Pack if he wants one. If he wakes up please tell him that I'll be in to speak with him tomorrow and that his presence is welcome with Cascadia."

Dr. Molinari inclined her head and left the room with one last nod to Nina. "I'll see you this evening, Nina."

Nina nodded, surprised.

"I know where the house is, Mr. Warden. I'll be there within the hour," Stoner said shortly. "This had better be worth my while."

"I hope so, too, Detective."

Stoner left with the human doctor and Lex grabbed the phone and made arrangements for Pack members to come and help with the newly changed werewolf.

On the ride back home Nina looked over at his face, which had tense lines etched into it.

"He can be trusted."

"I hope so, Nina. If he can't, I've just thrown the Pack into chaos and made it dangerous for us all."

"You have to tell him. You've involved humans in this whole thing and more than just with one crazy Pack member getting into a bar fight. This is essentially terrorism against them. If you don't deal with the human authorities you're going to turn them all against you."

"Against *us*," Megan said from the backseat.

"Uh, yeah. About that, Molinari says she's going to see me later tonight? Just what does this thing entail?"

"It's a ceremony. Most of the Pack will be there to welcome your wolf."

Nina stiffened and shut up. She didn't want the rest of the Pack there. She wasn't sure she even *liked* the rest of the Pack.

"Nina?"

"Not now. We're here and you need to deal with Stoner." Her body language was sending him the message not to mess with her and he warred with himself for several moments.

"Will you accompany me when I brief him? You have some information that we need to share with him and you can explain it better than I can."

"Don't sound so enthusiastic."

"Are you trying to pick a fight? I'm trying to include you."

Megan heaved a sigh from the backseat. Lex pulled into the garage and jammed the car into park. He turned to face his sister and Nina scrambled out of the car and into the house. "Do you have something to add?" he demanded of Megan.

"Lex, you are one of the smartest people I know. You're compassionate and generous but you are so stupid when it comes to women!"

"What does that mean? Why are you all so damned mysterious?"

"We aren't! You are so dense. Lex. Nina is really intuitive. Haven't you noticed that? She doesn't just blather on like so many people. She watches and listens even as she disarms people and keeps them off balance with her sharp comments. But she's very observant. I bet you she can tell you what everyone in that hospital corridor was wearing, whether someone was walking with a limp or not, if someone was hiding something."

"I know that. That's why I asked her to be there when I briefed Stoner. I thought she'd be pleased I was including her."

"Lex, the voice you used was tense and you were annoyed as you said it. Have you not noticed that despite her tough exterior, Nina is a bit insecure?"

"I was annoyed because she wasn't telling me something. And she's not insecure, she's defensive. I never know where I stand with her."

Megan shook her head at him. "Did you notice the way she reacted to the news that the whole Pack would be there tonight? Lex, the Pack stood there while someone tried to kill her. No one helped her. While you've explained it and she has accepted the Pack way for the most part, she can't have the warmest of feelings for us all because of it. Oh and hello? She's going to transform into a wolf for the first time in a few hours. That may be just a teeny bit stressful."

She got out as he did and put her arm around his waist as they walked toward the door. "And you do know where you stand with her. She adores you, Lex. I've never seen you this happy, even your agitation is happy. She's your equal and she's not afraid of you like those other females were. You're not insecure or you wouldn't pop off to each other the way you do."

He rolled his eyes as he opened the door. "Damn it, Meg, you're the smart one."

"Yeah, I know."

He chuckled and headed in to deal with his mate.

* * * * *

When he walked into his office he saw her there, back to him, looking out the window. He crossed and stood behind her, his body barely touching hers. He bent and kissed her neck and she sighed sweetly.

"I do really want you to be here when I talk to Stoner. You'd be helping me," he murmured into her ear.

She turned into him and put her head on his chest. His arms closed about her body. "How much do you want me to say?"

"Just follow my lead. Cade will be here as well."

She tried to move back but he pulled her tighter against him and kissed her forehead before letting her go.

* * * * *

Ben Stoner approached the house with a casual air but it was clear he was taking in every detail. Lex appreciated that about the man. He was observant without being outwardly judgmental.

Dave led him into the office, where they'd set out some beverages at the table rather than have Lex sit behind his desk. Now was not the time to make anyone feel like they were trying to outrank anyone.

Cade, Lex and Nina all stood and Stoner snorted and waved them all down. "Let's cut the shit, shall we? Get to the point."

Lex smiled and they all sat and he laid out the basic story about Carter, the gambling debts and the now-missing vaccine.

"We have our own problems with crime, Detective Stoner. He's absconded and has given something very important to less than trustworthy elements in our society. Nina has gone through his computers and we've got a basic idea of what happened, but where we are right now is finding out who's got the remaining vials of the virus and getting them back before anything else happens."

"I can't believe you have organized crime." Stoner's voice was laced with disbelief.

Cade shrugged. "You have your criminal element, we have ours. It's not something we like to advertise. I hope you understand that our telling you all of this entails a great deal of risk and trust on our part. We do it to protect weres and humans too."

"Last week, I had to attend a conference on murder crime scene investigation in Portland. I can't begrudge you a few criminals when we've got so many of our own. Unless and until it becomes an issue of safety, I will keep as much of this as I can to myself."

"We appreciate that very much." Lex inclined his head in the way the other Pack members did to him to show respect.

Lex then went on to outline what they were doing to locate the virus and the wolves who'd stolen it. They had trackers on it as they were all speaking.

"I want to be there when the final takedown occurs." Stoner leaned back in his chair.

"Detective, it could be very dangerous to any human in the area. I give you my word that we'll notify you the moment we capture the wolves responsible," Lex cautioned him.

"Don't make the mistake in thinking that was a request, Warden." Stoner turned to Nina. "And I think you'd want to be as far away from this as possible after what happened to your house and shop." He narrowed his eyes. "And your brother. Where is he, by the way?"

Lex growled when he saw Nina's slight wince, but she held it in well. "It's okay, Lex," she reassured him. "Detective, I believe my brother is dead and I believe the wolves who torched my house and shop are responsible. I think he heard something or they thought he did. In any case, I'm not letting go until they're held responsible for what they've done." She held her head high and her voice was steady as she said it.

"Fair enough. I apologize for upsetting you. But if you don't mind my asking, why did you become a wolf after all they've done to you?"

"Detective, what matters now is that I am a wolf. I am Second in this Pack and these wolves are my responsibility. I don't shirk my responsibilities."

Pride surged through Lex at her answer, at the way she accepted not only that she was a wolf but her position as well. He noted Cade's posture straighten in response too.

"Duly noted, Ms. Reyes. I can respect that." He turned back to Lex. "I'll be expecting a call before any takedown of these wolves takes place or I may feel like you haven't held up your half of the bargain."

Lex narrowed his eyes and finally nodded his agreement.

Stoner stood, they all shook hands and he left.

* * * * *

Lex checked in with his people at the hospital and those investigating the whole Carter mess. When he finished up some hours later, he went to look for Nina. He found her in Cade's room.

His adrenaline surged when he first caught sight of her curled in his brother's arms but he met Cade's eyes above her head and saw the anguish and concern there. He heard the soft sounds of her breathing and could smell her tears in the air.

"She's asleep," Cade murmured.

Lex crossed the room to where they were sitting. "What is it?"

"She's scared, Lex. Worried she won't do a good job as Second. Unsure of her transformation. She doesn't want to fail. Not you, not me, not the Pack."

Cade stroked a hand over those chocolate curls and gave a wry grin when he caught Lex staring at the movement. "She didn't want to worry you. She came to ask me about the transformation ceremony tonight. She just crawled into my arms when the tears came. Nearly broke my heart."

Lex knew that a part of that urge on her part to seek comfort from Cade was that he was her Alpha, and that would have been reinforced by his also being the Anchor. Still, it wasn't easy to see his mate in his brother's arms, asleep and exhausted from her tears.

Cade stood easily and put her into Lex's arms. She snuggled into his chest and sighed. "I wish I knew how to help her," Lex said softly.

Cade chuckled. "You do. She's yours. You're hers. Just be her mate, Lex, and the rest will work out. She's something so very special, but then you are too. Things will be easier after the transformation. It's the unknown she fears. It's ironic that you'd get a woman who is even more of a control freak than you are."

"Ha, ha." Lex rolled his eyes. "Hey, Cade?"

Cade tipped his chin up in response.

"Thanks."

"No problem. If it weren't for this pesky mate thing and you being my brother and all, I'd steal her away in a minute."

Lex stifled a derisive snort. "You wish."

Cade sighed and shrugged. "Yeah."

Lex started to reply but thought better of it. Instead, he took Nina to their bedroom and tucked her into bed where she slept as he worked and kept an eye on her.

* * * * *

Warren Pellini stared at Jack Reed in horror. "You what?"

"We infected the human but he got away. My men weren't watching closely enough. Before they noticed someone had called the cops and they'd picked him up."

"You lost a drugged up transient human who'd been infected and beaten up? Who are these wolves of yours, Jack?"

"They aren't anything anymore. There's only one left alive and he won't be for long. And the human was so tranked up that he won't remember anything. If he lives at all, that is. We don't know if it even took." Jack tried very hard to repress any nervousness. They were both alphas in their own right but Warren Pellini was insane pure and simple. On top of that he was utterly merciless.

"I'm beginning to see just why Carter was so frustrated with you wolves, Jack. What kind of disorganized organization are you running here?"

Jack wanted to explain that his wolves were used to running small time crime—nothing like kidnapping and human experimentation! But he knew excuses would just make him look weak.

"It'll be handled. I'll see to it personally. This bum has nothing on us. Chances are he's dead anyway."

"And if he isn't?"

"He'll be a wolf and we'll be sitting on a goldmine that will have the humans paying through the nose for years to come." Jack smiled through sharp teeth.

Warren watched him through dead eyes, seeing him for the liability he was. "Get the human back, Jack. We can't afford exposure at this stage."

Chapter Ten

ഇ

"Beautiful, are you ready?" Lex murmured, lips against her temple.

She looked at him in the mirror, meeting his eyes. She took a deep breath and nodded.

The house was filled with Pack. She could smell them all. Forest and loam. She scented power and family. Anticipation.

"I can feel them. Smell them."

He smiled as he took her in, dragging his eyes down her body, now clad in a midnight blue silk robe that she'd drop once they got outside under the moon to change. She was all curves and sex. Her scent filled his nose. He no longer smelled Pack, he only scented her. His mate. The particular mix of musk and pheromones that was his woman. It was alluring and seductive. Heady and intoxicating.

"They're here to welcome you home, Nina. I know this is hard for you. That you don't trust them much. But they're yours. I'm yours. Hell, even Cade is yours. Forgive them and they'll follow you into hell itself." He smoothed his hands down her arms, having to repress his urge to pull her down to their bed and make love to her for hours.

She took a deep breath and nodded. "I'll try."

"You're going to do just fine, beautiful. Your wolf knows what to do. It's not hard or scary. Just let it happen."

She heard a knock on the door and Cade opened it and walked in. He was shirtless, like Lex, and wearing low slung sweat pants. *Man oh man*, they were both so beautiful. He caught her appraising gaze and winked and they both laughed.

Lex made an annoyed sound and pulled her closer. "That's enough of that."

"You all should wear clothes then." She turned and kissed him quickly. "Okay, let's do this, shall we?"

Cade held out a hand and Lex another and she took both and let them lead her downstairs.

The entire Pack, minus the wolves who were at the hospital, was waiting. Anticipating their arrival. There was tension and excitement in the air and Nina felt slightly nauseated as her wolf stretched out inside of her body, readying to be freed.

As she passed the wolves all went to their knees. Cade and Lex led her outside and into the tree line that abutted the house. They stopped beneath a large maple tree and the Pack circled them.

Looking up into the clear autumn sky, Nina felt the pull of the moon. Felt the tidal sway of nature, felt her wolf respond.

"Let it happen, Nina."

She looked into Lex's eyes and watched as his humanity slid away. Watched as his wolf began to manifest. She felt a deep tug and looked to Cade, who watched her silently. He squeezed her hand and took a step back. Lex slid her robe from her shoulders. The evening cloaked her as the silver of the moon bathed her skin.

She raised her hands toward the sky and felt herself—her human self—simply go elsewhere and her wolf surge to the surface. She fell to her knees and watched in fascination as her body suddenly wasn't the same. She had four legs. She felt her nose and mouth as a muzzle. Wondered at the feel of her long tongue as it moved over sharp teeth.

From deep within her a sound of joy, of discovery and transformation, burst through her and into the evening air. A howl that echoed against the house and trees. Her howl was joined by Lex's and Cade's and the chorus of howls of the rest of the Pack.

The world was black and white. Sharp and vivid. The air was filled with a banquet of smells and sounds that she'd never noticed before. The earth under her feet was spongy and received her weight differently than she'd ever perceived it before.

She shook herself and took off at a run. Lex joined her, a wolf the size of a freaking pony, and bumped against her. She knew instinctively that it was playful and she shoved back. He grinned at her with those sharp teeth and yipped.

They ran and ran, playing and jumping through the forest for hours until Cade and Lex guided her back to that big maple tree. Once back, she dropped to her belly and crawled to Lex.

He grabbed the back of her neck with his teeth then let go. When she opened her eyes, the world was color again and he was holding out her robe.

Cade was ushering the others back toward the house and it was just the two of them under the stars.

"Such a beautiful wolf," Lex murmured. "How did you like it?"

"It was incredible. I don't even know how it all happened or even how I got back to this shape but I want to do it again." She had a smile on her face and Lex laughed.

"We will, beautiful. Now, let's go back inside so I can make love to you properly."

"You have a deal." She took his hand and followed him.

Before they'd reached the back deck, Dave rushed out and Lex's relaxed posture changed immediately.

"Dr. Molinari called. The transformation went fine until the Rogues showed up and took the new wolf and..." His voice broke.

"Tell me," Lex's voice held authority then and Nina felt the compulsion of it in her bones. She saw Dave's anguish and understood that something very bad had happened.

As Lex had demanded that Dave tell him the rest, he'd ushered Nina back into the house and was putting his pants on quickly.

"Brian is dead. They used silver shot. Eric is being treated right now for some pretty bad wounds. Charlie may not make it. He's in surgery."

Lex took long strides to their bedroom and pulled out a shirt and a bulletproof vest. Dave helped Lex get it fastened at the sides and Nina moved to get jeans and her Doc Martens on.

Lex looked up as he strapped a holster to his thigh. "What the fuck do you think you're doing?"

She fastened the Velcro at the sides of her smaller vest that Dorian had given her earlier that week. "I'm putting on a vest to go under my shirt." She pulled a sweatshirt on over it and undid the trigger lock on her handgun, checked the clip and put it in the underarm holster that she'd strapped on.

Lex grabbed her arm and pulled her to a stop. "I don't have the time or the patience for an argument now, Nina. You are not going. You will stay here. Period."

"I am Second in this Pack, I can shoot. I am a damned good fighter and I'm going. I'm not going to argue with you so that shouldn't tire you out. Now let's go."

"Dave, wait for me downstairs. Call Stoner and tell him to meet us at the hospital." Lex said it without taking his eyes from Nina. When Dave had gone Nina simply held up her hand.

"No. I'm not arguing with you on this. I am coming. I won't be stupid but I'm coming."

"You *are* being stupid, Nina. You are not trained to do this. I'll be distracted worrying about you."

"I'll stay back. I won't get into something I can't handle. But I'm not staying here and that's that."

"Damn it, Nina! You are not coming! Stop being such a stubborn female!" He shouted all of that but Nina heard the fear in his voice.

She reached up and kissed his chin. "I'm coming. I'm not getting hurt and neither are you. Please, Lex. These people murdered my brother, they took him from me. Don't make me stay back here. I need to be there. I need to see this through." Her eyes pleaded with him and her voice showed the depth of her emotion. "Now come on." She turned and walked out. He growled, following in her wake.

"Cade, order her to stay back," Lex called out as they entered the living room.

"I'll make every day of the rest of your life a living hell if you do," Nina called out as she grabbed her hair, twisted it up into a quick bun and secured it with a ponytail holder.

Cade stood there with a smile on his face and shrugged at Lex. "She'll be fine. She'll just follow you like a puppy if you don't take her. This way you can at least know where she is at all times."

"Some Alpha you are," Lex snarled as he checked the clips in his weapons and strapped them on while Dave helped him with the knife sheath at his waist.

Cade chuckled. "I like walking without a limp. I'm more afraid of her than you."

Nina laughed and went to the door and waited.

"Damn it." Lex stomped to her and pulled her shirt up and made sure she'd fastened the vest correctly. He rechecked her weapons and gave her a last look before shoving her out the door, knowing she was wearing a smug smile even when he couldn't see her face.

Triumphant that she had won, she wasn't stupid either. She knew that Lex was an expert at this stuff and she had no plans of doing the stupid heroine thing and getting herself trapped and endangering everyone else. No, Nina sat quietly in the car, listening as Lex gave orders to his men on the way over to the hospital. She had every intention of listening to and obeying his orders. He appeared to be partially mollified by her behavior, which relaxed them both a bit.

When they arrived the men fanned out on his orders and he headed toward Stoner, who stood similarly suited in a vest and weapons.

"What's the story?" Stoner barked and Lex quickly filled him in.

One of the members of Lex's team ran back toward them, still in wolf form. When Stoner noticed a panicked look flashed over his face. Nina touched his arm. "It's okay. He tracks better this way. He can pick up the scent of other wolves."

Lex looked deep into the wolf's eyes and nodded. He gave quiet, terse orders to the group. "They had a car and shoved the new wolf into it. But they didn't drive far and whatever it was they drove, it was unusual, so Shane kept the scent. They are two miles from here. We're going to take the patch of woods behind the hospital and approach the house from the rear."

Stoner nodded and spoke quietly to the two officers he had with him.

Lex approached Nina and looked into her eyes. "You will stay behind Megan. You will not hesitate to use your weapon on any wolf or human who attacks you. You will not run off or do anything stupid."

Nina nodded solemnly and then with her fingertip drew an X over her heart. "Cross my heart and hope to wear granny underwear until I die."

He choked a surprised laugh. "Nina, I have to know you're taking this seriously." His voice was urgent as he held her upper arms.

"I am. I promise you, Lex. I'm bitchy, but I'm not dumb."

"I love you." He kissed her forehead and she watched as he dropped the face of her mate and pulled the Enforcer mask on.

She took a step back in awe a bit of fear. He was so intense at that moment, strong and powerful. A killing machine. It was kinda hot.

He turned and made some movements with his hand and she watched as his men took their places while she took hers behind Megan.

They moved through the woods quietly. So quietly that it shocked Nina. Apparently when she became a werewolf she got wicked mad ninja skills too. She stifled an amused laugh, knowing that Lex would so not appreciate her levity at that moment. Her ears were very sensitive, her muscles fluid as she moved. She felt more aware than she ever had, noticing every sound in the trees, differentiating between birds and small rodents, even two deer that watched them all from a safe distance.

She realized that she'd begun to take being a werewolf not necessarily for granted, but simply as a fact. She would deal with it because it was now her reality and it was what she had to do both to survive and to stay at Lex's side. Moreover, she felt the responsibility to the Pack in a way she couldn't have understood before she transformed earlier that evening. For whatever reason, she truly *felt* Second. She felt responsible for the wolves in Cascadia Pack. They were hers and in a very real way, she was theirs. Even if she still didn't quite know how to get around what happened at the Pack house when she was attacked.

After a few minutes they approached the house. The lights were on inside and the back of the house faced the woods. From the tree line they could see into the living room. There were three men sitting in front of a television and one in the kitchen. A BMW 800 series sat in the driveway, not a very usual car, even in BMW-happy Bellevue.

Lex didn't say a word. His face was impassive as he directed his people with hand signals. He looked over at Nina and gave one hard shake of his head. She knew he was ordering her to stay out there and she nodded. He looked to Megan and gave her the palm of his hand—she was to stay with Nina. Megan inclined her head and backed Nina up into the trees a bit further, but they still had a view of the house.

Nina watched, holding her breath, as they headed out. While the other guards on Lex's team fanned around the house, he, Dave and Stoner walked straight up the back deck stairs and kicked in the back door. He was impressive and scary and Nina watched in awe as he did his Enforcer thing. Something deep inside her responded to how he moved, how he took charge. And she had to admit that knowing he was doing part of this whole thing to avenge Gabriel's death touched her deeply. There'd never been anyone in her life she could count on, on that level. Having Lex made her whole. Made everything all right even if it still brought a lump to her throat each time she thought of how pointless Gabriel's death was.

Lex shot two of the men in the head before they'd even stood fully. Stoner stood off to the side, weapon drawn just in case. Nina gasped as one of the wolves jumped at Lex, knocking him off balance but not off his feet. He was all violence and menace as he moved with liquid speed and threw the other wolf into the glass and out onto the deck.

There was a short struggle, but Nina's attention was torn from the scene by the sight of two men running toward them. Megan drew and one of them turned and saw her and jumped on her.

The other turned and moved toward Nina, growling and snarling.

It was time for her to do her job as Second. The weight of that fell on her until time slowed. With great clarity and a sense of purpose, Nina reached out, sighted down her arm and squeezed the trigger. The sound exploded, the acrid scent of gunpowder hung in the air around them. In an odd sort of calm, she squeezed again, and one more time, and the man crumpled to the ground.

She felt a touch on her arm and looked to see Megan speaking to her but she couldn't hear anything but the ringing in her ears. Her shoulder hurt, her eyes burned. Megan put an arm around her and squeezed. Nina had done her duty to her Pack and she'd saved her life and the life of her sister-in-law in the bargain.

Remembering Lex and the battle on the deck, Nina spun just in time to see Lex heading toward them at top speed. Fear on his face, he looked at Megan, who smiled and nodded, and he closed his eyes for a moment. Relief clear on his face, he moved to pick Nina up and cradled her against his body, holding her there as they walked back through the forest.

By the time they'd gotten back to the car she had her hearing back and his heartbeat was keeping time, lulling her.

He set her down next to the car and unlocked it. "Beautiful, are you all right?"

Nina sat down. "Yeah. I think so. I really don't like shooting people, Lex."

"I don't like you shooting people either, Nina. But you saved Megan's life. You saved your own life. You did what you had to do and I'm proud of you for it. You're strong and I'm thankful." He knelt in front of her and ran his hands up her legs and put his head in her lap for a moment.

She ran her hands through his hair. "Did you get the virus?"

"We got two vials. Jack Reed, the Alpha of the Rogues, is dead, his people in the house are dead. Our wolf was gravely injured, they took him to Dr. Molinari. I hope he makes it."

"What about Pellini?"

Lex shook his head. "He denied any involvement when I called him earlier and you know we couldn't find anything concrete tying him to any of this."

Megan came out of the woods and Lex went off to speak to Stoner and the guards for several minutes before coming back to the car and taking them back home.

"Is Stoner okay with what happened back there?"

Lex nodded. "He understands our need to run our affairs. He's going to be a liaison between the Pack and the police. I think it's a good plan. He's a good man."

Nina nodded. "Yeah. It'll be good to have him on our side."

Cade was waiting for them when they walked back inside. He hugged Megan and then Nina, kissing her lips gently. "Go take a shower, baby. You did good."

She smirked up at him. "Easy there, Mayor McTouchy."

Lex tugged on her ponytail with a laugh. "I'll be up in a few minutes."

She stood beneath the spray and let the tears come. Big gulping sobs shook her body. It was over. The men who'd killed her brother were dead and her mate was the one who made sure of that. Lex protected her and avenged her loss. The depth of what that meant stunned her.

Nina realized that being with Lex, even through all the horror that she'd experienced, had enabled her to get through it. That was family. *That* was connection.

It would take a while but in time, she would get over what happened in the living room of the Pack house. Eventually, she'd come to forgive the other wolves their inaction. She would however, use her position to deal with the stupid way werewolves treated humans. She'd do it for Gabriel and for the Nina Reyes who wasn't human anymore. Knowing that it would agitate the hell out of Lex and Cade just made the thought even more delicious.

* * * * *

When she walked out of the bathroom a dozen candles lit the room. Lex lay in the center of their big bed, the golden glow of the candlelight making him look godlike.

The corner of her mouth hitched up even as her body tightened in response to his presence.

"Hey there. You look happy to see me." She nodded to his erection.

"Yes, my *thingy* is quite pleased."

Nina laughed and jumped on the bed where he caught her easily and rolled so that he was above her, looking down into her face.

She reached down, wrapped her hand around his cock and squeezed gently. "I think you're old enough to say cock now, Lex. Sheesh."

He laughed and kissed her quick and hard. "Well, I *am* just a fuck-drunk werewolf, remember?"

"Oh yeah." She snickered. "Come on in, Scooby. The water is fine and your wife needs some action."

"I love you Mrs. Scooby." He positioned the head of his cock just outside her pussy and pushed into her body slowly.

"Good. Now shut up and fuck me 'cause I love you, too. You big tool."

Their laughter died on a gasp as he entered her body fully.

Also by Lauren Dane

ം

About the Author

꿍

Lauren Dane been writing stories since she was able to use a pencil, and before that she used to tell them to people. Of course, she still talks nonstop, but now she decided to try and make a go of being a writer. And so here she is. She still loves to write, and through wonderful fate and good fortune, she's able to share what she writes with others now. It's a wonderful life!

The basics: She's a mom, a partner, a best friend and a daughter. Living in the rainy but beautiful Pacific Northwest, she spends her late evenings writing like a fiend when she finally wrestles all of her kids to bed.

Lauren welcomes comments from readers. You can find her website and email address on her author bio page at www.ellorascave.com.

Tell Us What You Think
We appreciate hearing reader opinions about our books. You can email us at Comments@EllorasCave.com.

Why an electronic book?

We live in the Information Age—an exciting time in the history of human civilization, in which technology rules supreme and continues to progress in leaps and bounds every minute of every day. For a multitude of reasons, more and more avid literary fans are opting to purchase e-books instead of paper books. The question from those not yet initiated into the world of electronic reading is simply: *Why?*

1. *Price.* An electronic title at Ellora's Cave Publishing and Cerridwen Press runs anywhere from 40% to 75% less than the cover price of the exact same title in paperback format. Why? Basic mathematics and cost. It is less expensive to publish an e-book (no paper and printing, no warehousing and shipping) than it is to publish a paperback, so the savings are passed along to the consumer.

2. *Space.* Running out of room in your house for your books? That is one worry you will never have with electronic books. For a low one-time cost, you can purchase a handheld device specifically designed for e-reading. Many e-readers have large, convenient screens for viewing. Better yet, hundreds of titles can be stored within your new library—on a single microchip. There are a variety of e-readers from different manufacturers. You can also read e-books on your PC or laptop computer. (Please note that Ellora's Cave does not endorse any specific brands.

You can check our websites at www.ellorascave.com or www.cerridwenpress.com for information we make available to new consumers.)

3. *Mobility.* Because your new e-library consists of only a microchip within a small, easily transportable e-reader, your entire cache of books can be taken with you wherever you go.

4. *Personal Viewing Preferences.* Are the words you are currently reading too small? Too large? Too… ANNOYING? Paperback books cannot be modified according to personal preferences, but e-books can.

5. *Instant Gratification.* Is it the middle of the night and all the bookstores near you are closed? Are you tired of waiting days, sometimes weeks, for bookstores to ship the novels you bought? Ellora's Cave Publishing sells instantaneous downloads twenty-four hours a day, seven days a week, every day of the year. Our webstore is never closed. Our e-book delivery system is 100% automated, meaning your order is filled as soon as you pay for it.

Those are a few of the top reasons why electronic books are replacing paperbacks for many avid readers.

As always, Ellora's Cave and Cerridwen Press welcome your questions and comments. We invite you to email us at Comments@ellorascave.com or write to us directly at Ellora's Cave Publishing Inc., 1056 Home Avenue, Akron, OH 44310-3502.

COMING TO A BOOKSTORE NEAR YOU!

ELLORA'S CAVE

Bestselling Authors Tour

UPDATES AVAILABLE AT

WWW.ELLORASCAVE.COM

Make each day more *EXCITING* With our

Ellora's
Cavemen
Calendar

✝ www.EllorasCave.com ✝

Discover for yourself why readers can't get enough
of the multiple award-winning publisher

Ellora's Cave.

Whether you prefer e-books or paperbacks,

be sure to visit EC on the web at
www.ellorascave.com

for an erotic reading experience that will leave you
breathless.

CPSIA information can be obtained at www.ICGtesting.com
Printed in the USA
LVOW06s1634220913

353564LV00001B/216/P